Evil Presence...

Hey, Mary, ever dance with the dead?

Her head began to swim. She felt dizzy, ready to pass out. Who was playing games on her? She wondered if perhaps she was suffering from jet lag; she'd once heard that high altitudes had adverse effects on some people.

An eerie feeling began to work its way up her spine until it reached the short hairs on her neck, which felt as if they were standing on end. She had the sudden, sickening feeling that someone was watching her. But who?

And there it was, at the far end of the parking lot. The sun reflected brilliantly off the new paint of a black Camaro.

SHIVERS™

Book One

Vampire Island

By Derek Storm

FamilyVision Press

New York

FamilyVision Press™

An imprint of Multi Media Communicators, Inc.

575 Madison Avenue, Suite 1006
New York, NY 10022

FamilyVision Press™ and Shivers™ are trademarks of Multi Media Communicators, Inc.

Typesetter, Samuel Chapin
Cover, Michael A. Hernandez, Jr.

Library of Congress Catalog Card Number: 93-071550

ISBN 1-56969-350-1

10 9 8 7 6 5 4 3 2 1
First Edition

Printed in the United States of America

CONTENTS

Introduction

Chapter 1   Feast of the Dead.....................3
Chapter 2   Blood Hunt.............................13
Chapter 3   Hidden Place..........................20
Chapter 4   Priest of the Dead....................24
Chapter 5   Missing Tourist.......................31
Chapter 6   Devil Worship.........................35
Chapter 7   Daughter of Satan.....................39
Chapter 8   Case Closed...........................45
Chapter 9   Spider's Web..........................49
Chapter 10   Life and Death........................52
Chapter 11   Voices................................57
Chapter 12   Sacred Ground.........................62
Chapter 13   Occult Talk...........................66
Chapter 14   Waiting...............................74
Chapter 15   Vampire Dreams........................79
Chapter 16   Searching.............................83
Chapter 17   Vanished..............................87
Chapter 18   Waiting for Baby Eddie...........98
Chapter 19   Lost Boat.............................103
Chapter 20   Nosy Neighbors........................108
Chapter 21   Evil Presence.........................110

Chapter 22	The Awakening	115
Chapter 23	Foul Demon	119
Chapter 24	Night Creatures	126
Chapter 25	Gossip	132
Chapter 26	911	140
Chapter 27	Devil's Deal	143
Chapter 28	Nightmares	151
Chapter 29	Black Arts	156
Chapter 30	Morning	161
Chapter 31	Billy Peters	165
Chapter 32	Calling Satan	173
Chapter 33	Reverend Moses	182
Chapter 34	Final Battle	187

Epilogue

Vampire Island

CHAPTER 1

Feast of the Dead

Somewhere in the Florida Keys, 1693

If it hadn't been for their small boat taking on water, the two Jesuit priests and their crew may never have stumbled upon the secret Indian ceremony.

Looking for souls to save, Father Menendez, his assistant, and their enslaved shipmates had spent days searching for the island with the strange name, an island of which they had heard but which didn't appear on their map. Until the urgency of their ship's leaking became noticeable, they had no luck in finding the settlement. However, after realizing they had to land and mend their boat, they began to steer toward the nearest island. As their boat moved closer to the island, they heard the singing and smelled the fire.

The Jesuits' shipmates were six English sailors who were participating in the mission against their best wishes. Since night was fast falling, they did not want to leave the shelter of their boat. They'd heard the tales of cannibals, vicious Indians, and other dangers that surrounded the Keys of the New World.

In fact, the seamen would have rather taken

their chances against the current and headed back to the mission. There they would be free to think about escaping to the first English ship that came their way.

"Why can't we leave the savages alone?" John Lee, the biggest of the sailors, asked.

"Because we have come to the New World in search of converts," Father Menendez replied with resolve. "We have come to this island to save lost souls."

"They look for gold," one of the other sailors snarled to his mate.

"Quiet, we seek to save souls," Brother De Aviles, Menendez's assistant, whispered, making the sign of the cross.

The symphony of chanting and singing voices swelled up around them as they neared the beach. Father Menendez's confidence in his mission grew stronger. Once they landed, he ordered the sailors forward.

Brother De Aviles, on the other hand, sensed impending danger in the air. But as Menendez's subordinate, he followed. It was no time to be saving souls, he felt. They'd be lucky to save themselves.

Their footsteps were silent as they walked through the sand wet from low tide. As they neared the Indian village, alive with activity, Father Menendez led the party, defiantly rigid in the face of the oncoming task.

At the outskirts of the settlement, the men slowed, surveying their surroundings. As they tuned in on the multitude of chanting Indian voices, their tentative feeling they were outnumbered became sure.

"Do not fear," Menendez said, turning to the others. "I believe we will see glory when we ask them to accept the Lord."

They crept up to a large mound which lay on the perimeter of the clearing where the Indians were performing their dance. What they saw beyond that mound disgusted them. A large group of Indians was carrying bones and decaying corpses toward a fire set at the center of the clearing. From it, the smell of singed flesh traversed the air to foul the island's pleasantly salty fragrance. As the arms of that stench wove around them, the island abruptly began to stink of evil. It began to stink as if hell itself had opened up beneath them.

The Jesuit priests from the mission of St. Mary watched in dismay as the Indians continued their dance around the fire, which they slowly realized was blazing from an open grave.

There could be no glory, no conversions, amidst this savagery.

As they watched, the two priests recalled a story they'd heard. A Father Juan Bautista de Segura and his eleven companions had been tortured and put to death by the band of Indians

they'd sought to convert. With the dance fierce-
ly raging before them, the details of that slaughter took on a bold new freshness.

The sailors became increasingly restless.
Though the Jesuits believed that true souls were
saved by the blood of martyrs, the sailors preferred to keep their blood safe. Each demanded
to be freed, allowed to return to the relative safety of the boat. But Father Menendez, beliefs
strong, refused and threatened to flog any of
them who tried to leave.

So they stayed, watching the dance grow more
frenzied by the moment. Father Menendez,
unaware of the significance of the dance, waited
for the right moment to intrude on it. Little did
he know that this dance would soon be in his
honor.

Still the bodies flew in the putrid night air,
giving life to the blaze that grew with every addi-
tion of the dead. Some of them looked as
though they'd been dried and preserved; yet others turned to dust and crumpled when they were
touched, and the Indians scooped up glorious
handfuls of the deceased and shoveled them into
the grave.

The men watched as legions of Indians from
neighboring islands came to cast their dead into
the pit, to dine and dance in the Feast of the
Dead, to rejoice in life after death. They partici-
pated with fervor, for many of them had waited

thirty years for this night, and many would wait thirty years more.

"We offer them salvation," Father Menendez whispered, a mere sigh in the roar of the surrounding voices, "and look what they do. *Sacrilege,*" he said, spitting out the word.

Though the Jesuits had devoted their lives to converting the Indians, learning the native tongue and customs, the two holy men now realized the magnitude of their quest, how little progress had been made. What was learned over centuries could not easily become unlearned. These Indians were, and would remain, unbelievers.

"Do you think they are cannibals?" Father Menendez asked.

"They are dancing the Feast of the Dead," replied Brother De Aviles.

"The what?" Father Menendez queried, watching an Indian lift a smoldering human leg bone into the air.

"The Feast of the Dead," De Aviles continued. "I have learned of it in writings and travellers' tales. A pagan custom. They don't teach us of it in our missions because they know it conflicts with our Christian burial rites. But it is a tradition here on these islands."

Father Menendez watched a young woman lift piles of decay into the fire. "What does the Indian name for this island mean?"

Brother De Aviles uttered something in response but his answer was lost in the mesmerizing drone of the singing.

"What did you say?" the head priest asked once again.

Brother De Aviles continued staring at the gruesome sight before him as he replied. "I believe the translation is Vampire Island."

Menendez let the words sink in like a weight in water. *Vampiro!* The Spanish word for vampire. It was an island of the undead.

As if reading Menendez's thoughts, Brother De Aviles said the word, two syllables that hung thickly in the night air: "Undead." He paused. "In truth, that is what they are dancing for. For what they believe, literally, is life after death. By offering their dead to the flames, they mean to give the dead everlasting life, raising their spirits from the grave. That, Father Menendez, is the purpose of the Feast of the Dead."

"We must stop it!" Father Menendez retorted, raising his voice.

Brother De Aviles shook his head. "They would only kill us if we try. We are on their sacred ground."

"What sacred ground?" Menendez screamed. "This is not a church! Christian ashes have not been scattered here!"

"True, Father," Brother De Aviles said as he patted the mound they were hiding behind.

"But this is a burial mound, and this is their burial ground. To disturb it would be a sacrilege to their dead."

"And what about that?" Menendez demanded, pointing at a young Indian who was carrying a skeleton and forcing it to dance a macabre dance of death as if it were alive.

"They are showing the highest respect in their belief, rejoicing in the resurrection. They are dancing with the dead, giving them life, and moreover, saving their souls through the Feast."

Then came bloodcurdling screams as the Indians spotted them behind the mound.

Discovered, trapped, Father Menendez stood, again defiantly rigid, cross raised, ready for martyrdom. Brother De Aviles prayed his rosary, awaiting certain death, hoping the end would be both quick and painless.

The sailors retreated and made for the boat, but the Indians were fleet of foot and closed the distance within moments. Soon there was nowhere else to turn; the Englishmen were at the Indians' mercy. They were herded toward the blazing fire.

"You see, Menendez!" shouted John Lee, the largest sailor. "This is what your cross gets us!"

Once they were before the edge of the open grave, Menendez kicked at the pile of bones, sending them skittering into the pit. "I mock you, soulless heathens! Men, stand your ground with honor and prepare for heaven!" He dropped his head and began praying for their souls.

But the Indians had sensed discord between the Jesuits and the sailors. They gave the sailors a choice: Renounce the Jesuits and their religion, dance the Feast of the Dead and live, or side with the priests and perish.

Faced with the unexpected choice, the sailors committed the final betrayal: the renouncement that would seal their fates. They stepped back among the Indians and laughed as the two priests were tied to stakes to be burned alive.

Through tears of both compassion and rage, Father Menendez looked at the sailors and shouted as the fire below him was lit: "May God have mercy on your souls, but first may He condemn you to walk this island in search of your souls for three hundred years until Mary herself releases you."

John Lee shook his head. "Anything's better that what's about to happen to you, priest."

Menendez soon felt the fires flickering beneath his feet, rising to his legs, then engulfing his body. With the passion of a martyr he cried out, "In death I leave this earth! You will not have that chance!"

In a breath that was carried up by the flames beneath him, drifting out into the island and sealing their fate like an enormous black cape, he whispered, "Only Mary can set you free."

And with that last breath, in the waning moments of his life on earth, he thought of Mary, the Holy Mother of his Church.

Flames raced up Brother De Aviles' robe. "May God forgive you all," he uttered.

As the flames extinguished the life of the second priest, a great storm began. The Indians, believing that Father Menendez's curse on the sailors had brought the storm, slit the throats of the six prisoners. But the sailors did not die.

The Indians fell back in awe and fear, bowing their heads to the unknown. John Lee, the leader, felt the slit on his throat and knew he should have been dead. And yet he seemed to be alive.

It was true. He was alive. He could move, think, and feel. Yet while he knew he had not perished, he could feel the winds of change stirring within him. His blood burned. His eyes shone like hot coals. He felt exhilarated, powerful...immortal.

"Kill the savages!" he shouted.

The sailors drew their swords, then dropped them. They no longer needed primitive weapons to kill their prey. Rather, they felt a primeval urge to wring the life out of the Indians with their hands and their teeth.

In a killing frenzy that matched the howling winds in its ferocity, the sailors killed and feasted on the bodies. Some of the Indians escaped, but the bloodthirsty merely howled with laughter as they fled. Where could they run? They would be prey for another day.

After their hunger was satisfied, they dragged what was left of the dead to the water and tossed them in. Compared to the carnage unleashed by John Lee and his men, the savage Indians now seemed innocent.

Not long after, dawn began to break, and the sailors knew it was time to sleep.

But most of all, with three hundred years laid out before them like a madman's map, there would be time to feed.

And so was born the evil that flourished on Vampire Island, where generations would be the food for monsters until one named Mary could set them free.

Blood Hunt

Somewhere in the Florida Keys, 1993

The isolated footpath through the scrub on Sawgrass Key wasn't easy to follow for even the seasoned traveler, and Hans Schultz was lost. Very lost.

"Can somebody help me?" he shouted in stilted English. He repeated his plea in German, then, remembering where he was, a far cry from the familiarity of Berlin, called out again in English, "Help!"

Hans was a long way from Berlin, indeed. But like many Europeans, he'd dreamed for years of setting foot on the divine vacation havens so often pictured in magazines and brochures. He'd finally made it to one of them—Florida's Key Islands—and now here he was, lost.

He loved to fish, and had been able to set out on a few of the big charter boats. He'd also enjoyed the Keys' slow life-style and quirky charm. But his vacation was coming to an end, and the pleasures he'd attributed to the island were now dulling as he wished only to get out of this mess.

He could have spent his last day in America with his back snugly fit against a pool chair, sipping Budweiser, but he'd simply had to get in just one more fishing trip. So he'd rented a boat, a small, private boat. His travel agent had warned him against wandering alone in a strange land, but the appeal of fishing in solitude had ruled out his better judgment.

At dawn Hans sailed into unfamiliar territory and left his boat in a small inlet. Now, after fishing in that desired solitude, the increasing shadows of the aging day made all the small inlets look the same. He began to panic.

What was north seemed south and west seemed like east. As the darkness spread, surrounding objects took on more alien and threatening shapes.

He wanted to leave, to transport himself back to the safety of his rented room, where a cab would take him safely to the airport the next day.

Hans didn't spot six desperate-looking men who were watching him.

John Lee's senses began to pulsate as the presence of prey moved nearer. He could smell and hear the fresh blood flowing through Hans' veins.

They'd heard the clumsy noises of the lost man: curses, pleas, snapping branches. As soon as Hans' predicament had become known they crossed over from the unnamed spit of land that was connected to Sawgrass Key at every low tide.

Low tide was the only time that the vampires

could leave their island prison, for those without souls could not swim across the saltwater barrier. They'd simply watch the ebb and neap tides carefully after dark, waiting for the opportunity to escape and hunt.

This was their only means of satisfying their unquenchable thirst for human blood. All they could hope to do was lie and wait when food— unsuspecting boaters and the occasional tourist. With the millions of tourists coming through the Keys each year, the authorities couldn't possibly be concerned with an unfortunate few who became the meals of starving vampires.

Strange things happen: boating accidents, abductions, fatal falls into deep pits. And they were about to happen again.

Hans had never been an outdoorsman—never chopped wood or camped alone—and he'd never heard the sounds of the dark Key's night that filled his ears.

"Hello!" he shouted nervously in his best English, hoping someone would hear him.

But no one answered. Rather, nothing human. The palm fronds rustled overhead. The tide slapped gently against the beach as it continued its soft withdrawal from the land.

He could feel the cool sand between his toes as he wandered in circles, still looking for his boat. The boat now represented a haven, somewhere to spend the night.

The sultry Florida night air continued to waft his scent to the vampires. They were closing in on the vulnerable mortal. They knew he was alone. In trouble. They needed his blood.

Stealthily they moved over the ground they'd trod for three hundred years.

To keep from panicking, Hans began humming a German folk song. *I wish I were in Berlin,* he thought as he began to search for shelter. If he couldn't find the boat, at least he'd find a temporary sanctuary, safe from the threats of the dark island. "I'll be okay," he muttered to himself over and over.

Get hold of yourself.

The sounds of movement in the bushes startled him. Six men appeared.

It was then that he realized the men were carrying lights, low, flickering lights that swung rhythmically from side to side. He did not know at the time that it was a lure the vampires had been using for hundreds of years to attract their victims like flies to a spider.

"Hello," he said, raising his hand in a nervous gesture of welcome. He started to move toward them.

As he did, what appeared to be a dark shape obscured his path.

A night and a path that were already black became even blacker. It was a darkness that bore no name, one that knew no description.

Whatever it was before him seemed to absorb light as if it were a cosmic black hole.

He cleared his throat and swallowed. "Excuse me, sirs, but my name is Hans Schultz, and I'm quite lost. Is there any chance you can help me?"

"Please," he whimpered. "I am lost. Can you help me?" His body was turning cold in the hot Florida air. Something was wrong. The silence made him uneasy. He began to fear for his safety.

The vampires now tightened the circle and closed in on their prey. They loved the hunt and the feel of a victim's fear filling the air.

"What in God?" Hans whispered as the dark images sharpened.

They were indeed men, but not really: dazed, filthy creatures with pale skin and hypnotic yet fierce looks. Their sharp broken teeth now shone against the lamplight.

For a moment, Hans was too terrified to move. Then he took flight, punching through the constricting circle of death.

"Kill him!" John Lee screamed.

There is no incentive greater than the fear of terrible death to get the adrenaline racing. Hans swung blindly, stumbling, tripping, as he battled to get away from them.

Surely there was someone else on the island who would help him. Surely this was not how

God had intended him to die. But all he heard in response to his pleas were the grunting noises of the night creatures in pursuit.

The vampires knew there was nowhere Hans could run, nowhere he could hide. Three hundred years on the Keys, they knew every square foot of the island. There would be no escape for Hans.

The German's blind frenzy surprisingly led him to water. Momentarily collecting his senses, he found he'd reached the lagoon. Not far from where he stood, his boat bobbed in tune with the softly moving waves.

With shaking hands outstretched, he entered the lagoon to just below his knees, and he stumbled onto his boat.

Quickly behind him, the vampires closed the distance.

As Hans fought to untie the boat, hands were suddenly gripping his ankles, his wrists, his neck. The more desperately he clung, the harder he was pulled toward the land.

Still he resisted, feebly fighting off the hands and blows that pummeled his body. Snarling, growling, guttural noises came from those attempting to block his escape. And like a victim in a crocodile's underwater death roll, Hans' strength gradually waned. How long could he struggle? How much longer could he endure the battle?

The vampires had nearly pulled him free from the boat. In his last dying effort, he grabbed on to the side of his small boat like a crying infant being torn from the arms of its mother.

His exhausted body and soul, bloody from bites and blows, defeated by terror, gave way. His red-smeared fingers clawed at the side of the boat, his fingernails scraping against the wet planks. The vampires would feed.

All that remained of Hans Schultz—a bloody handprint on the side of a beached boat. And now that too, damaged and capsized, was inching below the water's surface.

When all that remained of Hans' body was tossed into the water, John Lee, well fed and sated, extended his hand toward the sinking remnant in a mock gesture of hospitality and whispered, "Welcome to Florida, my friend. Welcome to Vampire Island."

CHAPTER 3

Hidden Place

The sleepy airport at Marathon, Florida, stirred awake as the scattered friends and relatives of the passengers on USAir flight 558 from Orlando saw the plane come into view. The ground crew, shirts and shorts sticky from the thickening humidity, prepared for its safe landing and quick departure.

It was the only airport between Miami and Key West. No one watching the slow movements of the ground crew would guess that tourists were something to anticipate. Like gnats in summertime, outside visitors were becoming a nuisance.

Sixteen-year-old Tina Tipton, a Coppertone beauty whose good looks turned heads, lifted her hair off her sweaty neck. The heat and the humidity were oppressive, enough to turn a sane person crazy.

Somewhere in the metal bird circling the landing strip sat Tina's cousin, Mary Knight, whom Tina had invited for the long-awaited Midsummer's Eve bash. The invitation had been made in June, when the weather had been at least mildly tolerable.

Midsummer's Eve was the teen party of the summer. Everyone stayed up and stayed out.

Otherwise, Tina might have left town herself. The heat in August was ungodly.

But as everyone knew, Midsummer's Eve was worth braving the weather. Everyone who could get out, or sneak out, stayed up all night, dancing and romancing. It was the most exciting evening of the year. Nothing—not first dates in parked cars, the prom or graduation—could compare to it. It was Homecoming Dance, the last day of school before summer let out, New Year's Eve all wrapped up in one glorious, naughty night.

Tina looked at the surrounding faces. Life had indeed changed in one generation. What had twenty years ago been a civilization of farmers and fishermen had been replaced by a tourist shakedown mentality. Many of the faces she did not even recognize, where it seemed just years before she did. Perhaps some did live there, others were leaving on the outbound flight. Tina knew who her friends and family were, and that was all that mattered.

The pilot of flight 558 blinked as the bright sun bounced off the control panel. "USAir 558 coming in," he said, closing off radio communication with the ground tower.

The whole of Marathon and its surrounding inlets were visible in the shimmering heat. The spectacle looked like one huge tourist postcard below the plane.

As the pilot concentrated on landing the plane, he scanned the islands beneath, thinking of his one true passion: fishing. He would reach back, and in a mighty arc, cast his line far out into the water, where the lure would attract swimming creatures, the sizes and colors of which he could only guess. He was and would always be a fisherman at heart, and he couldn't wait to reach his secret place.

He was now trying to find it, the place he'd spotted on a previous lay-over. It was an unmarked jut of land that looked like an island at high tide.

It sat off by itself, away from Sawgrass Key, as though God himself had snipped it from the mainland and saved it just for him. *Hope they're biting,* he thought.

"Let's take her in, Captain," his copilot said, interrupting his fantasy.

As he directed his attention to the strip below, he caught a distant movement out of the corner of his eye. He snatched only a fleeting glimpse out of his side window, but for a moment, he thought he saw a capsized boat bobbing near his special place.

As the plane began its descent, the captain spoke to his copilot, his eyes still straight ahead. "Gonna get to do some fishing this time. Gonna get to my island."

"That one you told me about?" the copilot

replied.

"Yeah," the captain said. "I've heard some of the locals call it Vampire Island. Don't know what would make them call it something like that. It's darn near the most beautiful thing I've ever seen. Heck, it's not even an island, really."

Soon after the big bird was down and running, the landing as smooth as skimming the top of soft butter with a knife. Within several minutes, the passengers were unloaded.

Once out of the plane, people cried out and shrieked and hugged. The overbearing sun hung above them like a heavy ball trying to tear through the fabric of the sky. It glistened off everything: the chrome of vehicles, the windows of the buildings, the tears of joy on faces.

Even off the bloody handprint on the side of a capsized boat near Sawgrass Key.

CHAPTER 4

Priest of the Dead

Jeremy Wagner looked at himself in the full-length mirror that leaned against the wall opposite his bed. Wearing only a pair of faded blue jeans, he admired his body, flexing his pectorals and biceps. He ran a hand through his silky, shoulder-length black hair.

"You are one bad dude," he said to the reflection.

He turned down the volume of his stereo, which was shaking the floor with Ozzy Osbourne. Walking over to his desk, he flipped through the Satanic Bible he'd ordered through the mail.

He'd been going over the material thoroughly, reading and rereading each passage, each word, trying to absorb the malignant energy of the text. Being the leader of a growing club of devil worshipers, he felt a need to know the literature inside and out, to be able to recite it in his sleep.

The club had been working out well. To the parents of the others involved, the club was just a bunch of longhairs getting together to party and crank loud music. It did not interfere with Jeremy's ultimate, glorious goal: to live forever.

It had all begun only a year before, when his parents had made him come with them on what he'd thought would be a boring trip to St. Augustine. But when he saw what was supposedly the Fountain of Youth Ponce de Leon had been searching for, he found his destiny, his purpose in life. He was young and full of the bright-eyed vigor of youth, and it had never occurred to him until then that people took death for granted. Everyone assumed they would die someday; it was simply a matter of fact. But what if there was a way around it? What if there was a way to party, pick up chicks, jam tunes, eat burgers forever? He'd been interested enough in the macabre throughout his youth to know that there were tales of the undead, roaming bands of night creatures who fed on the living so that they could live forever. He liked the idea of a life without death.

He turned and sat in the center of the small circle of rocks he'd set out in the middle of his room. "This should double the power," he whispered, proceeding to recite a black prayer he'd memorized.

Up to this point, Jeremy had been working on a curse to place on a kid at school who'd been taunting him. After all, great leaders could only go so far on rhetoric; there came a time when they had to show their power.

Nothing seemed to happen and Jeremy was disoriented. The curtains did not begin to flap, the lights did not dim, he did not feel a rush of air as the unholy swam by him.

"What the hell?" he said to the room. "I must be missing something."

Being a self-professed Priest of the Dead was more difficult when one lived at home. Conducting his rituals almost always required a locked door and loud music, as well as a deaf ear to the beckoning of his mother. Once his father came home from work, it was impossible to do anything but read the texts quietly. At this moment, his parents had packed up and left town on business, and two weeks was ample time to exercise his craft to its fullest. With parental barriers removed, he'd hung Satanic symbols throughout the house, symbols he'd seen and admired in the stack of books and magazines he kept beneath his bed.

Things had indeed been fine the first couple of days they'd been gone, but it wasn't until he received the letter that he knew the cherubs of darkness were blowing their trumpets for him. The letter had been a flyer, signed by both the sheriff and the high school principal, warning parents of a reported increase in cult activity, including a checklist of "How To Tell If Your Child Is Into Cults." It ended with a paragraph stating that "The most difficult problem law enforcement has across the country is with the lone, self-styled Satanist or someone just experimenting with cult life."

He'd swatted a fly with the letter then burned it.

He walked back over to his desk and began to flip through some photocopies he'd made of old Jesuit diaries he'd found in the library. The copies included entries from the missions in the early years of Florida.

"If they only knew," he said to himself. "The sheriff would have a heart attack."

One of his black arts manuals had prompted him to research the diaries. It had said that a disciple of darkness should study the Jesuit ways if the disciple wished to know the enemy better. Ironically, the enemy had done him a favor.

Among the documents he'd found an entry concerning the death of Father Menendez, a report that had been passed on by one of the few surviving Indians. One particular line from the entry was emphasized in bold type: The line had been spoken by Menendez himself: **"May God have mercy on your souls, but first may He condemn you to walk this island in search of your souls for three hundred years until Mary herself releases you."**

Jeremy nodded in appreciation. If the writings about the Key Indians' Feast of the Dead were accurate, and if the old Jesuit maps were correct, then the undead might be living right now down the road. He'd heard the myths of creatures of the night inhabiting remote areas of the island, but as of yet nothing had been proven. After all, he believed he could unlock the secrets of eternal life. Surely he was fit to seek the undead stalking the night.

Besides, Jeremy thought as he continued to flip through the copies, a flurry of disappearances had been unaccounted for, like that German tourist, for instance. There had been a blurb at the bottom of the front page recently reporting that a German man had rented a fishing boat and failed to return it. As far as Jeremy knew, the man still hadn't shown up.

So was the idea of the undead—of vampires—so crazy?

If the legend of the Feast of the Dead was indeed true, then the next one was about to happen.

He chuckled to himself. Sometimes in life things had a way of working out that went beyond mere coincidence: One, his parents were gone for two weeks; two, Midsummer's Eve was approaching at the three-hundred-year mark of the Feast of the Dead.

Three, Mary. Mary Knight, Tina Tipton's cousin. The one she'd told him was coming to visit.

"Until Mary herself releases you," he whispered, licking his lips.

Gathering the papers and arranging them into a neat stack, Jeremy figured that if there were vampires nearby, and if they were yearning for release, then he just might be able to offer them a girl named Mary, along with a variety of other edibles suitable to fit their tastes: the teenagers of Sawgrass Key.

The whole idea of the Feast of the Dead began to take on new importance. His chants, prayers, and words to the dark spirits had all been for naught in his quest for life eternal. A determined man had to explore all his options. If there were in fact undead roaming the Keys, and if their moment of release was near at hand, would they let him in? Would Mary and others be the admission to their dance?

It was worth checking out.

He heard the sound of a passing plane. He looked up at the ceiling of his room.

"That's Mary's flight," he said, grabbing a black T-shirt on his way out to his car. The airport was only minutes away.

"Mary, Mary, quite contrary, how does your garden grow?"

He started the car and backed out of his driveway.

Soon he was speeding to the sounds of AC/DC.

Devilish thoughts flashed through his mind. Then a particular image came to mind. The image of Tina Tipton.

She'd taken a liking to him lately, and he

knew it. In fact, she'd recently said she'd do *anything* for Jeremy.

There was certainly something he wanted her to do now.

He'd planned a party of his own on Midsummer's Eve, a private bash on the beach exclusively for club members.

He would soon inform Tina that she was to be the escort of a very special guest. A very special girl named Mary.

CHAPTER 5

Missing Tourist

Tina Tipton licked her lips, trying to gloss them. She flipped her hair and turned from them, looking for her cousin amidst the unloading passengers. All around her, people were rushing to greet others; she was waiting for her turn to put on a sentimental showcase when Mary came into sight.

"Hey, Tina," someone said.

The boy in front of her was Billy Peters, one of the locals who went to her high school. Unlike her opinion of most of his gang, she found Billy to be rather sweet.

"Hi, Tina," he said, wringing a Florida Marlins baseball cap in his hands.

She smiled at him. "Hi, Billy."

"Gosh, it's a hot one today," he said.

She knew that Billy had a crush on her, and she knew that his insecurity made him uneasy around her. She tried to lighten the load on him a bit.

"Sure is, Billy. I don't envy your having to work in this heat. It's too bad you can't get to the pool or the ocean or something."

"Aw, shucks," he replied, kicking at the ground. "There's plenty of time for that. I gotta work to save money for college."

"Oh? Where are you going?"

"My parents want me to go to Florida State, but I want to go to the University of Miami. Where are you going?"

"Someplace local," Tina replied, turning away from Billy to scan the crowd.

He could tell he was losing her.

"Hey, Tina, have you heard about that tourist who's missing?"

"Lose one, win one, isn't that what they say around here?" she replied, shrugging her shoulders.

"This one's different, though," he said, hoping to capture her attention. "He rented a boat from my uncle and didn't bring it back."

"That's what the police are for," she replied.

Billy tried to say something, but Tina spotted Mary emerging from the plane. She started to move away from him.

"Nice talking to you, Billy. Gotta go."

"There's a reward if you find the boat!" he yelled as she left.

She stopped for a second. "For the tourist?" she asked.

Billy shook his head. "Ain't worried about the tourist. My uncle just wants his boat back."

"Nice guy," Tina said, and turned away from him again.

Billy shrugged his shoulders. "Talk to you later."

Tina kept walking toward the plane. While she was excited to see her cousin, her mind floated back to the tourist for a moment. She'd read about him in the paper, the same paper in which Jeremy Wagner had learned about the missing person. She'd been relatively unaffected by the story, given the fact that missing persons were not highly unusual in the Keys. But a feeling of unease had crept up on her like a spider scrambling up the leg of a chair.

Sheriff Diggs will probably find him drunk down in Key West.

Yes, that was certainly a likely possibility. Most of the missing persons were in fact people from out of state who drank a little too much and then set to wandering unfamiliar territory.

Then she saw a black cabdriver sitting with a leg hanging out of the open car door. Tina thought she recognized him.

Things aren't what they seem around here.

She stared back at the cabdriver, whose gaze was on her. He took a drag from a cigarette and blew the smoke out in a long cloud toward her.

The tourists see Florida one way, but just below the surface in the Keys is something really different. Different like Jeremy's crazy Satan stories.

"That's it!" she exclaimed to herself, making the cabdriver widen his eyes. She'd seen him at Jeremy's meeting the week before.

She knew her feelings about Jeremy had been

growing, even though he was into some *really* weird stuff. But there was a magnetism, a dark attraction, that drew her to him. Perhaps it was because he was so free, so passionate about his ideas. There was a wild side, a gritty edge, to Jeremy that Tina had been unable to resist. He was so much more interesting than most of the other boys on the island.

The cabdriver moved, interrupting her thoughts. He tossed his cigarette onto the pavement and snubbed it out with his foot.

"Crazy Haitian," she said to herself. The look on the cabdriver's face made her believe he'd heard her.

For a moment she wished she'd never met Jeremy Wagner. What had started as a strange crush on an eccentric boy was potentially dangerous. His preoccupation with her, his preoccupation with her attending all the meetings was turning into an obsession.

Still, she could not let go of her feelings for him. She knew she could not escape. He had a hold on her heart.

"Tina!" Mary shouted.

Tina put Jeremy and Satan behind her, and she ran toward her cousin with open arms.

CHAPTER 6

Devil Worship

It had been a good thing Jeremy had allowed his relationship with Tina to develop before suggesting that she come to a meeting. If he had let the cat out of the bag too soon, he surely would have lost her.

So he'd played it cool. He'd talked to her in the hallways at school, sat with her at lunch, and spent extra time with her. It was during these precious moments that he'd earned enough trust to at least feel confident enough to ask her to come. If she freaked out after all of that, well, then, she was never going to buy into it anyway. But for some reason, the vibes he'd received told him that she would not call him a freak and run. He had been able to sense his growing influence on her. It was in her eyes, her face, the small way she stirred whenever he approached.

And so he had asked.

And so she had come.

He'd taken her to a closed-down gas station a few minutes away from the business district, down near the bridge. He remembered her anticipation, her budding excitement at the unknown. "What exactly do you do at your meetings?" she had asked. He had merely smiled at her and put an arm gently around her shoulder. "Tina," he'd replied. "We simply get together and *groove*."

The gas station had been abandoned for well over two years. Cardboard boxes were stacked and smashed along the walls. Old tires leaned against another. Someone had hung an old sheet to separate the old office from the room where Jeremy conducted his meetings. The old sheet still hung, now with the symbols he and the others had painted on it.

Jeremy had become aware of a new ability: He had found he could communicate with other people at times without moving his lips. It was as though he could speak and listen to his disciples by merely sending and receiving thoughts. It didn't work with everyone: he'd tried it on his mother and father and only received an "Are you feeling okay, son?" But the mind communication was especially strong among his group.

He'd found that his effectiveness in mindspeak was growing stronger with Tina too. She didn't really know it yet, but she was slowly becoming one of his followers, and becoming one of his followers meant that one was taking a bizarre step from reality into the unknown.

She'd found it both terrifying and fascinating. She'd watched as the ceremony started. She'd absorbed it. There was something intriguing about the occult because it was a violation of a society that prided itself on order, correctness, regimen.

But most of all, she liked Jeremy's wild side. There was a neon DANGER sign hanging from his neck, blinking on-and-off, on-and-off. It made her tingle.

She'd calmly viewed the decorations: black robes with multi-colored symbols, religious banners tacked on the ceiling along with a ripped-up choir robe bearing the symbol of the Marathon First Baptist Church, a worn-out, soiled mattress in the corner.

My God, she thought. *Does he sleep here?*

It was at that moment that she'd begun to recollect all the tabloid horror stories, all the details of a host of talk shows that probed the occult. She'd recalled tales of young people entering these groups and never coming out.

It was then that Jeremy had almost lost her. She'd risen to leave but he'd gently held her arm.

Please, he'd said to her without moving his lips. *Please don't go. Stay. Stay for me.*

She folded her arms across her chest as though suffering from a sudden draft. Her common sense told her to split, to blow doors on that place. But Jeremy's pleading eyes had met hers, and she'd begun to remember the kind, gentle moments with him: the words of calm, of understanding, or warmth. And looking into those eyes, she knew she could not leave.

Jeremy kissed her forehead in gratitude. Then

he left and re-entered moments later wearing a long, black robe with a pentagram over his heart.

The congregation began chanting from their Satanic bibles, some of them banging baseball bats against the floor like prehistoric savages.

"Tonight, my friends," he said with renewed vigor. Tina's decision to remain had enlivened his spirits. "Tonight we will commune together."

Tina's head swam as someone draped a black robe around her. She was slipping away from herself.

She was Alice in Wonderland falling into a pit of dark images where nothing was as it ought to be. Was she falling into sympathy for the devil and asking to go to hell?

She thought of her mother, her friends, her life at school. What mattered to her most, however, was love.

And for love, she was willing to fall.

CHAPTER 7

Daughter of Satan

"Tina!" Mary Knight squealed.

"Mary!" Tina screamed back.

The two girls embraced each other.

"My goodness, it's so good to see you!" Tina said, holding Mary's arms out in order to get a better look at her. "My, my, girl. You do look *fine!*"

"You don't appear to have gotten any uglier yourself," Mary replied, wiping a stream of perspiration from her face. "Wow! Is it hot here."

"Get used to it," Tina said, gesturing to her surroundings. "I live in it."

They looked at each other in silence, smiles on their faces.

"There's so much to talk about," Tina finally said. "It's been so long."

"I know," Mary said. She broke into an even wider grin. "Give me another hug."

"Excuse me! Miss? Excuse me!" A flight attendant was coming down the plane's stairs holding a hairbrush.

"Oh my gosh," Mary said, looking down at her carry-on bag. The zipper was almost all the way open. "I'll bet a bunch of my stuff fell out. I'd better go back and make sure I didn't lose anything."

"Okay," Tina replied. "But hurry up."

Mary scooped up her bag and began to jog toward the plane.

Tina watched her as she went. How much her cousin had grown. The last she'd actually seen her was...could it have been ten years? Mary was surely a beautiful young lady.

Then she felt him. She could feel his eyes on her. His thoughts in her mind.

I see she's arrived, she heard him say in her mind.

Startled, she began to turn around in circles to locate him. She couldn't find his face among the moving crowd. Her hands rubbed her temples.

Go away, she responded with her thoughts. *How are you getting in here?*

I'm in there because we groove together, my darling.

A hand on her shoulder almost made her scream.

"What are you doing here?" she asked through her gritted teeth.

"Relax, sweetheart," he replied, rubbing his hand on her arm softly. "You act as though it were a crime to be seen with me. No one here knows you're a DOS."

"A DOS?" she said, confused. It sounded like it had something to do with computers. She was happy yet irritated. The sight of him in his T-shirt, muscles bulging, hair flowing, made her tingle. But he had chosen the wrong time to surprise her.

"Daughter of Satan," Jeremy grinned. "I made up the term myself. Pretty cool, huh?"

"I guess," Tina shrugged, feeling more uncomfortable. "Please be careful what you say. Someone might hear you."

"No one heard me," he said.

She turned, and Jeremy followed her gaze toward the airplane.

"Your cousin here?"

"Yeah."

"Have you told her about the meeting on Midsummer's Eve?"

"No," she said, a feeling of unease welling up inside her. "Why do you want her to go so badly?"

"I want her to be *with* us, to find the way to eternal life."

Tina shrugged again, keeping her eyes turned from him.

"You will talk to her, won't you, Tina?" she heard him say, his voice tugging at her heart. It was full of hurt at the prospect she might let him down.

"Just give it some time," she replied with resignation. "It's not something you get into over the phone, you know."

"I want you to bring her," he said. His voice turned cold.

"We'll see," she replied. "Just chill."

You have to make sure she comes, he projected into her mind.

Tina blinked. The bitterness in his voice jolted her. He was usually sweet. He was strange and had a lot of problems but had always been kind. It was that kindness that had motivated her to follow him into acts which she'd never deemed herself capable of doing.

And now this business with her cousin Mary. Why had he become interested in Mary? She wished he'd get off her cousin. She wanted to be alone with her, absent of Jeremy.

"Tina?" he beckoned.

A part of her wanted to run and embrace him, another wanted to spit at his feet.

He must have been able to sense her mixed emotions, for his anger was becoming hard to contain. He did not want any static. He wanted this all to go smoothly.

"You think she'll like me?" he said, hoping to strike a chord with her.

And if she does, will you be jealous? he taunted her with his mind.

She finally turned to face him, scowling.

"Leave me alone, Jeremy Wagner. What you do from now on is your own business."

"And what you do is mine," he replied, winking at her. He sneered. "See you later, DOS."

He flipped his hair over one shoulder and

began to walk away. Tina wasn't sure what bothered her more: the fact that Jeremy was showing a side she'd never seen before or the fact that she'd felt her feelings begin to shift away from him. At that moment, she didn't care if she ever saw him again, and that realization jarred her.

Tina looked at the plane, wishing Mary would stay on and fly back home. Would keeping Mary around place her in harm's way?

She obviously couldn't just send her home. She was going to have to find a way to calm the storm. Maybe if she took Mary to only one of Jeremy's meetings, that would appease him.

But somehow she didn't think so.

There was Midsummer's Eve to think about. After all, that was one of the main reasons Tina had invited Mary at this particular time of the year. Jeremy's party was the same night, and Tina didn't think he would view their absence with much understanding.

She glued her eyes to the plane, waiting for Mary to re-emerge.

It'll be okay, she thought to herself. Everything will work out fine.

Jeremy walked out of Tina's eyesight and stood in the shadow of a large tree. He pulled a cigarette out of a crumpled pack and stuck it in his mouth.

"I'm losing her," he thought. "Pretty soon I'm not going to be able to trust her."

He dragged on his cigarette, taking a full cloud into his lungs. He blew it out.

"Gotta get a better hold on her or she could be bad news."

He pulled the cigarette from his mouth, closed his eyes, and concentrated on reaching her mind.

Midnight. Be at my house at midnight. Do you understand, Tina?

He focused his attention on the response the air would carry back to him. He tried to hear her thoughts and picked up an ocean of sounds instead: cars, horns, other voices, a dog barking. In the midst of it all he could pick up the vibes of the angry, the hurt. Whose thoughts he was receiving was anyone's guess.

Then, swimming up to the surface of the ocean, he heard a girl's voice, a faint answer:

Yes.

He smiled, placed his cigarette back in his mouth, and moved toward his car.

CHAPTER 8

Case Closed

Cruising the back road at the other end of Marathon, Sheriff Amory Diggs swerved out of his lane as he noticed a coffee stain on his shirt.

"Damn," he whispered. "That donut shop oughta be shut down, serving that paint as coffee."

He stopped his car on the shoulder and put it in park. He found a crumpled Kleenex on the littered floor of his vehicle, spit into it, and began rubbing at the stain.

"Diggs here," he said into the handpiece.

"Got another call from the German Consulate in Miami," a woman's voice replied. "They're still howlin' about the missin' tourist."

"Jumpin' jackrabbits. I already told them I've driven Highway One from Big Pine to Islamorada. Tell you what. Why don't you tell them keg-tappers that their boy is probably dead drunk on the bathroom floor at some strip bar. Better yet, tell them he probably met some Madonna and ran off to get married."

The call operator at the station chuckled. "They think that Key Largo and Key West are a block apart."

Sheriff Diggs laughed. "You tell them this ain't no movie set down here. Cryin' out loud,

Key Largo's a couple long hours in traffic from Key West on a day like today."

"I know that, Sheriff. But they're stone stubborn. They want their boy."

"Well, get back on that phone and tell them that if they promise to get me a couple cases of German beer and some sausage, I just might put in a little overtime."

He jimmied open his glove compartment and pulled out a pack of Lucky Strikes.

"'Fraid I can't tell 'em that, Sheriff," the operator said.

"Well you'll think of somethin'. Just get those jerks off my case."

"Right. Ten-four."

Sheriff Diggs put the handpiece back on its hook and lit a cigarette.

"What a pain." He took a drag, then coughed up some phlegm and spit it out the window.

"I ain't no baby-sitter! I'm a respected officer of the law, dammit!"

He scratched his belly.

"Let them call the feds."

He threw the car into drive and swept back onto the road.

"Missing persons. I'm sick of missing persons. Those idiots ever hear of maps? Jeez!"

He couldn't count the number of calls that'd ended in the retrieval of lost tourists from bars, ditches, motel rooms with hookers, boats where they'd passed out from too much booze. He'd taken the job because he'd fallen in love with the law from all the years watching *Dragnet* and *Highway Patrol.*

But he did know that if one really set one's mind to getting lost, the Keys were a good place to start. It had become a rather popular spot for criminals and scum on the run. Though there was only one road leading from Miami to Key West, there were a myriad of side streets, back streets, and mean streets where a person good or bad could easily get lost. Disappear for good, even.

Being an officer of the law, he was aware of the multitude of persons reported missing each year. And being an officer in Florida, he knew that the state had a fair-sized slice of the larger cake. He'd heard all the stories about disappearances in the Bermuda Triangle, and he knew people liked to swap tales about visitors from outer space deciding to make a pit stop in order to grab a couple of Americans to go. There had even been a tidbit here and there about witches, Satanists, and vampires willing to snatch a body or two when the need arose.

"Well, they can all kiss my behind," he said, swerving to avoid a grungy dog that'd wandered into the road.

If only Sheriff Diggs knew that the time spent at the coffee and donut shops he frequented would have been enough to reveal an item of particular relevance. Like a boat that'd been rented by a tourist and not returned. A boat rented by a German tourist.

A boat bobbing just off the highway he was driving on, in a lagoon, hooked to the scrub trees. Not far away.

A boat with a bloody handprint on it.

He pushed the pedal to the floor and turned up the volume on his radio.

CHAPTER 9

Spider's Web

The two USAir pilots stepped down onto the baking pavement of Marathon.

"Nice landing," the copilot said, smacking the captain on the back.

"That's what they pay us for," the captain replied, grinning. "Man, is it hot. Sure would like to grab a six of Bud and hit the fishing. Want to go?"

"Nah."

"Got some time due me," the captain replied, checking out a tall blonde walking by. "Want to get in some fishing. I think I found my spot."

"You and your spot. You act like all the fish in the world been hanging out waiting for you to find your *spot*. Fishin's fishin' as far as I'm concerned. Don't matter if it's in the Gulf or in a watering hole in someone's backyard."

"Well, my friend," the captain said, taking a step in the direction of the blonde. "You obviously don't know much about fishing."

"Well I couldn't go with you anyway," the copilot shrugged. "I'm booked back doing puddle jumps up the coast to Jacksonville."

"Tough luck, amigo. Guess that means I'll have to catch six then. Five for me and one for you."

The copilot wandered away to talk to one of the flight attendants, leaving the captain to observe the crowd by himself.

Not far from where he was standing, Tina Tipton stood on her toes, straining to see her cousin over the heads of the crowd.

It had been ten years since Mary had moved away from Marathon. Back then they'd been little girls concerned with dolls and ice cream. They'd written letters, and they'd talked on the phone many nights, but how was Tina to act now they were face-to-face? So many changes had taken place. Tina had not seen Mary mature, had not been there when Mary'd shunned golden Barbie for a hairbrush and lipstick. What was she really like? What kind of boys was she attracted to? How would Mary react when Tina told her about Jeremy?

She began to play with her options in presenting her story about Jeremy. Should she tell Mary how he came to capture her heart? Or should she confess and tell Mary she'd fallen for a Satanist?

What should I do? she nervously thought.

A few more people came down the ladder leading from the exit. Mary was not among them.

Tina looked around and breathed a sigh of relief when she didn't see Jeremy. She was growing impatient now.

"Where are you, Mary?"

The makeup she'd so laboriously applied that morning was beginning to run. Her hair was growing heavier as beads of perspiration formed at her temples.

She imagined herself in the center of a spider's web, its fine threads reaching out to everything around her. One thread represented the troubles of young love, where an immature heart is often misled. One reached out to these days of summer passing by at high speed. Another led to her family, now distant strangers to her adolescent mind. And on the web a hairy black arachnid inched toward her, trapped and helpless. And what chilled her to the bone, what scared her most of all, was the attached to the pincers snapping in anticipation of eating her alive was the face of Jeremy Wagner.

CHAPTER 10

Life and Death

The muggy summer breeze oozed through the trees lining the gravel road that led to the clapboard church. A few miles away, young girls and boys ran about in tight shorts and T-shirts, spilling beers and bouncing beach balls. A middle-aged couple sat on a beach in solitude, holding each other in a lover's embrace.

But those who had walked as far as a country mile to hear the city preacher speak thought not of love or drink or money. They'd come to hear talk of God, of good, and of evil.

The Reverend Moses continued his sermon as several more people filed in to fill the oak benches in the back of the church.

He raised his Bible before the wide-eyed crowd.

"And it says right here, in the Holy Scripture, in Ephesians, 'For we are not contending against flesh and blood, but against the principalities, against the powers, against the world rulers of this present darkness, against the spiritual hosts of wickedness in heavenly places.'"

His captivated audience, waving fans to cool their perspiring faces, murmured in agreement.

"Hear the Holy Word! The serpent still slithers in our Eden! Look into your hearts, and ask yourselves if you have been tempted to eat from the tree! Look into your hearts, and decide if you have the faith to stand up against the Legion that works against your Lord!"

"Hallelujah!"

"I hear you, my brother!"

The reverend stepped down from the podium and walked to an elderly black woman sitting in the front pew. He closed his eyes and put his hand on her shoulder. She raised her head toward Heaven and closed her eyes, her face wrinkling and splitting like worn, cracked leather.

"My sister, have you seen the evil?"

"Yessir," she replied, beginning to rock forward and back in her seat.

"My sister, have you felt the evil among you?"

"Yessir." A tear ran from the corner of one eye, cutting a wet trail over her rough skin.

"And, sister," he said, his voice gathering strength. "Is that evil not all around you?"

"Yes!"

He lifted his hand gently from her shoulder and turned to the man sitting beside her. Putting his hands on the man's knees, he bent over till their eyes met.

His voice lowered so that only a few up front could hear him.

"And you, my brother, have you seen what lies beyond the present darkness?"

"I've heard it, Reverend, and I know it's there, but I ain't never seen it."

Reverend Moses turned and jumped back up to his podium.

"This Satan of which I speak does not chase girls in movies! This Satan of which I speak carries guns, and drugs, and venereal disease, and liquor, and all the things that attach us to this world! This Satan is in our children, who live their lives with abandon, thinking they will never see the dirt of their graves!"

"Yes!"

He took a step away from the podium and walked around to the front of it.

"My brothers and sisters, who have come here today to hear the words of a man who has traveled long and far, and seen more evil and sufferin' than one deserves in a lifetime, hear me now. Hear me and listen if you never believe a word I speak again. We're all gonna die. *We're all gonna die someday.* And when that day comes, only you and you alone will stand before your Judge, and only you will be able to look back on your lives and see if you bought into the lies that evil told you. Nobody in flesh lives forever, and that's what I'm here today to talk to you about."

"Is Satan here?" a little black girl two rows back said in a soft, angelic voice.

Reverend Moses chuckled warmly.

"Yes, my sweetheart. Yes, he is."

He averted his eyes from her to scan his audience. "I have roamed this country of ours, and I have learned to smell evil. It smells, it does. And when I came here, I smelled it like meat that'd been sittin' out for two weeks."

"I seen it," the elderly woman he'd touched spoke.

"What did you see, sister?"

"I seen some things, some devil things, on the island seen only at low tide."

"Go on."

She covered her face with her hands, the images tearing at her.

"I seen things that looked dead. Like they shouldn't be alive. Things carryin' lights, and they was swingin' 'em back and forth, back and forth."

"And when did you see them, sister?"

"I saw them last night, Reverend. When I was fishin' in my skiff near the bridge. I wouda tole Sheriff Diggs, but he wouldn't believe an old colored lady, anyhow."

"That's right!"

"He don't listen to no colored folks!"

Reverend Moses stepped back and turned to look at the statue of the crucified Christ. Being a man of God, he believed that evil was not a physical manifestation but rather flourished in the hearts of humankind, the worst monsters of all. He'd lost his brother to the evil of the human heart, and it had been his brother's despair that had driven him to travel the country in his fight against Satan. His brother, a heroin addict, had found voodoo in New Orleans and had come to believe that spiritual trickery would give eternal life. In an attempt to prove his invincibility, he'd jumped from an apartment building to his death.

Reverend Moses did not believe in the monsters of comic books and movies, but he was aware of the stories passed through the ages telling of agents of the Dark Lord, Satan's henchmen.

If in fact the lady spoke the truth, and if in fact there were sons of Satan, on a nearby island, then he had reached the end of his road. He would be able to stand before the soldiers of the army who'd stolen his brother's life, and he would be able to send them back to Hell in the name of the Lord. Even if it meant his own death, he would prove that only God is eternal.

He turned to face them.

"Hold hands, brothers and sisters. Hold hands and be strong, and may God be with you."

He closed the Bible on the podium and led them in a prayer.

CHAPTER 11

Voices

"Can I help you?"

The voice startled Mary, and she bumped her head against the bottom of the seat under which she was retrieving several small items that had fallen out of her carry-on bag.

Rubbing her head, she looked up to see a blonde flight attendant smiling at her.

"No," she said, shoving a keyless fluorescent green keychain into her bag. "I think I've found everything."

While on the plane, her thoughts had been preoccupied with the unease she felt in visiting Tina after ten years of separation. She'd failed to notice her bag had fallen over, spilling some of its contents.

What could she say? Mary felt estranged from Tina. Their families had become distant after Mary's had moved away. Her aunt seldom wrote, let alone called, and their fathers, once good friends, had not spoken in at least five years. Mary had missed a huge chunk of her cousin's life and she felt an awkward void between them. Perhaps they would have fun after all, talking about boys, tanning in the sun, partying on the beach on Midsummer's Eve. Perhaps she would be able to return home knowing she'd renewed an old friendship.

Returning everything to her bag, she left the plane. A couple of the boys working down beneath the plane whistled as she stepped off the stairs.

"Creeps!" she shouted.

The boys laughed to one another and continued with their work.

Like her cousin had been doing for several minutes, she stood on her toes, hoping to see Tina's head over the shuffling crowd.

"Mary!"

She'd been spotted.

The two girls pushed their way toward each other and picked up where they'd left off.

"So, how was the flight?" Tina asked as they walked toward the luggage area.

"Fine," Mary replied. "But they showed a movie so stupid that I started reading the airplane safety manual."

Giggling, they waited at the luggage area.

"There's my bag," she said.

With bag in hand, they walked to a gate in the fence separating the parking lot from the tarmac. As Tina, a few steps ahead of her, was fishing in her purse for the keys to her car, Mary heard the voice for the first time.

Save any souls lately, Mary?

Mary stopped dead in her tracks. She glanced around the parking lot, but only saw a small ocean of sparkling chrome and steel.

Hey, Mary, ever dance with the dead?

Her head began to swim. She felt dizzy, ready to pass out. Who was playing games on her? She wondered if perhaps she was suffering from jet lag; she'd once heard that high altitudes had adverse effects on some people.

She shook her head and began following Tina, who was already at her car, opening the trunk.

"Hurry up, slow poke!" Tina yelled.

"I'm coming, I'm coming," Mary replied sluggishly. Her feet were beginning to feel like someone had poured cement in her shoes. Her suitcase felt as if it were three hundred pounds.

An eerie feeling began to work its way up her spine until it reached the short hairs on her neck, which felt as if they were standing on end. She had the sudden, sickening feeling that someone was watching her. But who?

We're gonna groove, you and me.

That did it. She was going totally lunar.

She dropped her bag and her fingers went to her temples.

Then, with an acute sense of hearing she heard the distant sound of an idling car. She spun around to try to locate it.

And there it was, at the far end of the parking lot. The sun reflected brilliantly off the new paint of a black Camaro. A boy with long black hair and sunglasses was leaning out of the window with his arm resting on the top of the door. He was too far away for her to make out anything particular, but she sensed he was smoking a cigarette and smiling.

"Tina?"

Mary stood transfixed, her eyes locked on the black Camaro.

"Tina?"

Tina grabbed Mary and spun her around. The expression on Mary's face told her immediately that something was definitely wrong.

"What is it?" she asked, grabbing Mary's upper arms. "You look like you've seen a ghost."

Mary was at a loss for words. She started to raise a shaking hand to point in the direction of the car, but when she looked the car was gone.

"What in the world are you looking at?" Tina asked.

Tina suddenly felt as if she had been doused with a bucket of ice-cold water.

"It was…it was…"

"It was what?"

"It was…nothing."

Tina picked up Mary's suitcase and heaved it into the trunk. She slammed it shut.

They both got in the car, and soon they were driving off to Tina's house.

"You're gonna get to see your fair share of slobbering boys around here," Tina said as she rolled down the window. "I swear, they've got one-track minds."

"Uh-huh," Mary replied, staring off into the distance of Marathon. Her mind kept hearing the voice.

Hey, Mary, ever dance with the dead?

For the first time in her life, she felt really, really scared.

CHAPTER 12

Sacred Ground

Jeremy pulled into his driveway and turned off the Camaro—the "Black Cat," as he'd so ingeniously named it—cutting off a Judas Priest tape in mid-shriek.

Once inside his house, he grabbed a can of beer from the refrigerator and ran up the stairs to his room. Cracking open the can and guzzling a few mouthfuls, he sat down at his desk before the mess of books, magazines, and photocopies.

His fingers went to the photocopies of the old Jesuit diaries. Now that Mary was safe in town, he could feel his plan gaining momentum.

His eyes went again to the Father Menendez entry, and he absorbed the details of the Indian's account as dictated by a translator:

From *Jesuit Travels in the Floridas,*
1660-1700, page 112.

The Indian boy confirmed that the tribes had been practicing the pagan Feast of the Dead that evening. He said this ancient custom taught that only by performing the ritual on a specific night on the thirtieth year from the last Feast would they ever be able to release the souls of the dead to fly freely to eternal life.

Because the dead were freed by being cast into huge, burning graves, the Indians had developed a system to accommodate the deceased during the intervening three decades. They'd begun the practice of digging temporary graves similar in form but smaller in scale. From throughout the Keys, Indians carried their dead in their arms, with ropes, on rafts, to lay them to rest on an island accessible only at low tide, the island they'd designated the Island of the Undead.

It was at one of these great feasts, in 1693 A.D., that Father Menendez and his crew met tragedy, a tragedy that ended in his curse of the men who'd betrayed him in his despairing final moments: **"May God have mercy on your souls, but first may He condemn you to walk this island in search of your lost souls for three hundred years until Mary herself releases you."**

Jeremy put the paper down and leaned back in his chair. The only sound aside from his heartbeat was the rustling leaves outside his open window.

Until Mary herself releases you.

Of course he knew that Father Menendez had

been referring to the Virgin Mary, the mother of Christ. But the fact didn't alter what he aimed to do.

He would wait until his party, his meeting, was underway on Midsummer's Eve. Those who cared enough about his purpose would forsake the other, larger bash for the deliverance he would promise. He would tell them he had found a passageway to the other side, a portal to eternal life. He would say he had been called forth by Satan in a vision, that he'd been woken by the Dark Lord in the middle of sleep. The Dark Lord had led him to the island seen only at low tide, and had led him deep into the trees where he found an entrance to a little cave. Satan had promised him that only the chosen were shown the cave, the entry to life everlasting.

His followers, his disciples, would eat the story up. They'd follow him like toy soldiers. After all, as far as they knew, Jeremy was special. He had the favor of Satan.

It would be then that the undead—if they were indeed on the island, as the diary indicated—would find them, and they would surely become excited at so much food at one time. Jeremy would stand before them and strike a bargain. He would promise them all the food they could set their teeth upon one condition: They take him among their kind and give him life eternal. If they complied, there was a bonus for completion of the deal.

Mary. He wasn't sure how eager they were to rid themselves of their predicament: whether they liked living forever or were sick of it, but there would still be the issue of Mary, a name that would speak volumes to those who'd been left hanging under a curse bearing her name. He would tell them he knew where she was and could offer her to them if they satisfied his requirement: Eternal life. He was sure that Mary would be a dead lock for the deal.

It was beautiful.

Jeremy slammed the rest of his drink down in three gulps and took off his shirt, throwing it onto his bed. After sliding a Black Sabbath tape into his stereo and cranking it full volume, he picked up a dumbbell and started doing biceps curls.

"Oh, Jeremy," he said in admiration of himself. "You are one *slick* dude."

CHAPTER 13

Occult Talk

Tina's custom-painted pink Mustang roared down the road cutting through the business district, music blaring from the windows.

"Aren't you afraid of getting a ticket?" Mary asked, feeling uncomfortable.

"Are you kidding me?" Tina replied, taking her eyes off the road to reach for a pack of cigarettes on the dashboard. She lit one and turned down the radio. "You ever see *The Andy Griffith Show*? That will give you an idea of Marathon's police force. Most of them are probably at the donut shop."

"This is a nice car," Mary said, still shaking off the fogginess of her fright.

"And you better treat it real nice," Tina replied, blowing out a lungful of smoke, "'cause I've got my life's savings in it."

Mary grabbed the door handle as Tina screeched around a turn.

"We've got so much to do and so little time," Tina said. "I still can't believe you're finally back."

"You've built this Midsummer's Eve into Mardi Gras," Mary replied. "It sounds like something right out of a movie!"

"It's the best party in all of Florida. Better

than New Year's Eve in Key West." Tina honked at a blue Honda she was tailgating.

"Tell me what else has been going on," Mary said. She was starting to relax a little, trying desperately to replace her unease with thoughts of the fun that lay ahead. "You sounded so mysterious over the phone the last time we talked. What's been going on? Find yourself a guy?"

Tina thought a bit before replying. Here was the crossroads she'd anticipated. Should she ease into the story or should she come right out and tell her?

"Boy, you're quiet," Mary said. "Come on, tell me about it!"

Tina decided to sidestep her a bit longer as she pondered her delivery.

"My summer's been great! How about yours?"

Mary decided to let go of the boy topic for now. There would be time enough.

She shrugged. "It's been okay."

"Just okay?"

"Yeah," Mary replied, slumping in her seat. "Not a whole lot to speak of. Just a lot of studying."

"What made you go to summer school anyway?"

"I already told you. I wanted to graduate high school early."

Tina cast a sideways glance at her cousin.

"Yeah, right."

"It's the truth!" Mary protested.

"NOT! You just want to follow Keith to California," Tina said, knowing full well that Keith was a touch-and-go subject with Mary.

"No," Mary said, staring out the window. "I'm over him."

"For real? I thought you two were getting pretty serious. You know, marriage and the whole bit."

Mary turned back to Tina, a serious look on her face. "It's over, okay?"

"Over, over?"

"Like dead and gone."

"Okay, so who have you been dating."

"You don't really want to know."

"Sure I do! Give me the juicy details! Like have you met any guys you wouldn't tell your parents about?"

"You think I'd tell *you*?" Mary teased. "You, Miss Gossip Queen of America?"

"Come on, you know I'd never tell," Tina replied.

"I've been out with a few boys."

"I don't know what the boys in Orlando are like," Tina said, "but down here you need to carry Mace on a date."

"I'll remember that."

Tina made a quick left and said, "You'd better have it branded in your memory."

They drove on for a few minutes in silence. Mary couldn't believe how much her past home had changed. As a little girl, she'd played in fields where supermarkets now stood. Places she'd remembered walking with her father to watch birds were now parking lots. The sweet home of her youth was becoming a tourist haven, a local's nightmare. It was nothing compared to what Disney World had done to Orlando, but it still gave her pause.

"Hold on!" Tina shouted as she floored the Mustang. Faces in slow-moving vehicles to Mary's right stared out at her in agitation. Tina, unfazed, started humming to the song on the radio.

"So what's been going on here in the Keys?" Mary spoke up, hoping to revive the topic of Tina's love life and slow down her driving. "Now that you've grilled *me,* you can tell who *you*'ve been dating," Mary said.

Okay, Tina thought. Here we go. "Can you keep a secret?"

Mary nodded her head in anticipation.

"Do you know anything about Satan?"

The question jolted Mary. She'd been expecting a tale of a budding romance, of flowers and kisses and everything. But Satan?

"Satan?"

"You know, the occult."

"Like in the movies?"

Tina nodded her head. "Well, it's kind of like that. But I'm talking about the real thing. Black masses. Pentagrams. Spirits."

Mary frowned. "Are you serious?"

Tina turned her head sideways. "Dead serious."

Mary looked hard at Tina, letting the words sink in. She'd heard of a small group of kids at her high school in Orlando that had messed with the black arts, and she'd heard the stories about heavy-metal bands' album covers, but this was her *cousin*.

"Well?"

Mary looked at Tina again. Contrary to her expectations, she was confronted with something that could cast a dark cloud over their relationship.

Tina cleared her throat. "Black cat got your tongue?"

"Do your parents know about this?" Mary managed to ask.

"Are you kidding? They'd flip if they knew I was messing around with it."

"Are you?" Mary asked, astonished. "What kind of messing around are you doing?" A cold shiver was running up her spine, and the feeling of creepiness she'd felt at the airport was returning.

"It's not *that* weird," Tina said. "It's a part of the culture down here. There are lots of groups involved with the occult. There's even an island the locals call Vampire Island."

"There is?"

"Yeah. Jeremy told me about it."

Jeremy. At least that cat was out of the bag.

"Jeremy?"

"That's my boyfriend's name," Tina replied. "But don't jump to conclusions. He's kind of cool."

"Cool? He worships Satan and you think he's cool?"

"It's a long story," Tina said, sorry now that she'd told Mary. "Forget it," she finally said. "We'll talk about it later."

Mary let the stuff about Jeremy go, but it stayed in her mind like a chunk of black mud. Her eyes glanced over the Gulf of Mexico in the distance. She realized she wanted to know more about what Tina was involved in.

"So what goes on in these meetings?"

"Lots of stuff," Tina replied, becoming increasingly uncomfortable with the subject. "There are plenty of things that go on if you know where to look."

Mary stared at her cousin. "What exactly are you saying?"

"What I'm saying is that there are lots of strange things on the island. Things that are cool and scary at the same time."

"Like what?"

"Enough for now," Tina said, hoping to close the door on the subject. "If you're so curious, there's a party on Midsummer's Eve where you can see for yourself."

Tina pulled into the driveway of her house. Mary stayed in the car as Tina stepped out. If nothing else had remained constant, at least her cousin's house had. It was exactly as she remembered it.

Stepping out, Mary spoke her thoughts. "Your house hasn't changed much," she said.

"Some things change, some things stay the same," Tina said, not knowing how true the statement rang in Mary's ears.

Yes, Tina. I understand that. But how much have you *changed?*

Tina and Mary retrieved the suitcase from the trunk and walked into the front door. Mary asked, "Is Aunt Elly home?"

Tina didn't answer. She turned her key in the lock and let herself in. "Are you coming in or are you going to stand in the heat all day?" She disappeared into the house, the screen door slamming shut behind her.

As Mary stood staring at the house, speculating on the strange events of the day, she heard a soft purring engine approaching.

Like she was in a movie, she turned her head in slow motion. Time seemed to elongate, seconds became minutes. The same black Camaro was creeping by, and the boy with the long black hair was staring at her, a wicked smile on his face.

Saved any souls lately, Mary?

Mary dropped her bag, and her hands flew to her mouth, which was agape with terror.

The boy floored the gas and sped off down the street. Mary could have sworn he'd been laughing.

"Come on!" Tina's voice cut through the air. Returning to her senses, Mary stood shivering in the sweltering heat.

She stepped out into the street and looked toward where the car had sped off. It was nowhere to be seen.

"I'm coming," she said, walking back to her suitcase. She picked it up and began to walk toward the screen door where Tina was standing with her hands on her hips.

Before she reached the porch step, Mary looked at an upstairs window. She saw a hand close the curtain.

Tina wasn't kidding. There is something really weird about this place.

Fighting desperately to keep her thoughts to herself, striving to ward off what she thought were wild imaginings, Mary stepped into the coolness of her cousin's home.

CHAPTER 14

Waiting

It seemed like clockwork, Jeremy's plan was working, coming together in perfect harmony.

He'd had to see her. He'd had to have a look at the human body that was to be the key to his dreams.

And, to his surprise, getting into her thoughts had been easy. When he'd first become aware of his ability, he'd thought it limited to the select few who'd travelled into dark spiritual life with him. The power within him was growing stronger. He didn't know exactly why he'd been able to send his thoughts to Mary, but the mere fact he could would be enough to make her recognize she was not dealing with some flake. Soon enough, she, like any mortal dealing with the forces of the unknown, would succumb to his unbridled power.

Now driving with both windows down, AC/DC pumping out of the speakers, he sped along Highway One. Summer wind streamed through his hair. The salt smell of the Gulf filled his nostrils. The vibration of the engine surged through his body.

His stomach tensed. His palms perspired. His breath quickened. He couldn't wait any longer. Like a little boy anticipating a big package at Christmas, he yearned to have the day arrive, to visit the little spit of land the locals called Vampire Island.

He kept the pedal pushed to the floor until he turned off down a dirt road which was one of the few outlets to the little island accessible only at low tide. He parked the car and got out.

Squatting down on his haunches, he waited patiently until the tide was low enough for him to cross. He hurried across and excitedly began to wander the beach for signs of life...or death.

Standing, he inhaled a dank smell and stared out at the Gulf stretching to the horizon.

He walked along the beach for several more yards. Momentarily settling in to enjoy the quiet pleasure of the island, he stopped and looked around him.

Then he saw them.

Several sets of footprints that started from where the water broke and led to the trees.

His heart started pounding.

This was too good to be true. First the legend, then Mary's arrival, now this. Knowing full well that no one lived on the island—only wandered near it to fish or swim—he hoped that these belonged to the undead he had wished for.

Now it would be his secret. The legend surrounding the island, the one passed by word of mouth in bars and streets and supermarkets, had cast a taboo shadow over the island. People rarely visited it. It had earned the same notoriety as a haunted house. The only souls brave enough to spend any amount of time on the island were usually tourists or foreigners ignorant of the stories attached to it.

His eyes followed the tracks and his feet followed. When he was at the edge of the dense growth of trees, he peered through, too nervous to enter. In the distance, he saw sand dunes. The more he focused on them, the more he began to sense that they were not merely dunes but mounds that had been deliberately built. Curious to check his facts, he reached into his back pocket and pulled out a folded piece of paper. It was one of the photocopies of the entries from the Jesuit writings. He began to read a footnote to the Indian boy's story of Menendez's slaughter:

> After the Indian boy had told his story to the interpreter and had it repeated to a Spanish officer stationed at the mission of St. Mary, which was near what is now Miami, a wave of rage swept through the Spanish leaders. The military was dispatched to the Keys and scores of Indians found near the island were slaughtered and hung. When the bloodshed ended, few of the Indians in the region remained. Those who did not perish fled inland.

All that remained was the island itself, which was scattered with a multitude of what appeared to be burial mounds. Research into the Indians' culture revealed that they invariably sought sacred ground above the high water-mark to secure their dead between the great Feasts of the Dead. Without the luxuries of mountains, caves, or abundant hardwood found within the Plains or the mountain states, the Key Indians were forced to use these makeshift burial plots.

Similar mounds were discovered during the building boom of southern coastal areas of Florida. Developers unearthed entire cemeteries. Most of what has been found has been either discarded or sold—a loss to our current drive toward understanding and preserving this unique culture.

Burial mounds within the mystical Island of the Undead remain unexplored.

Jeremy folded the paper back up and returned it to his pocket. Each new discovery reaffirmed his thoughts, strengthened his plan. He knew the time to meet the undead was close at hand.

Pleased with himself, he turned and walked back to the bridge of land joining the islands. Before he crossed, he noticed a slight movement out the corner of his eye. He turned toward it and began walking toward a lagoon obscured by the surrounding scrub.

He stopped at the edge of the lagoon, a wicked smile spread across his face.

A capsized boat drifted—nothing *totally* unusual about that.

But on the side of it!

He saw the bloody handprint, the desperate graffiti of someone who had suffered.

Oh yes. This is good. This is very good.

Jeremy crossed at low tide and walked back to his car. Stopping to look back across the island, he wondered where the vampires were and if they dreamed.

CHAPTER 15

Vampire Dreams

Yes, Jeremy, sometimes vampires dream, too.

John Lee stirred in the crevice he'd found in the old reef formation that marked the top of the island. During their three hundred years, the vampires had searched every part of the island for places to hide from the cursed daylight. Unlike legends and movies, there were no caskets buried deep in cellars of old, dusty houses. All they had were their graves, little caves, crevices like the one in which John Lee restlessly slept, to serve as sanctuary during the forbidden hours.

What does a vampire dream? Of necks? Of food? Of blood dripping richly from a vein?

For John Lee and his crewmates, there was little left to relish during their time of rest. The thoughts and images that dominated their sleep prior to their curse were a thing of the past. No more did they experience the thought of beautiful women, the smell of the open seas, winning great fortunes. Their insatiable appetite, the burning hunger had become their sole purpose for living and had stamped out the passions of normal life.

In its place was a life without end. They'd lived three hundred years hunting, eating, and hiding with no end in sight.

In a different time, in a different state of mind, John Lee might have been able to grasp the fears that had given birth to the legend of the vampire. For what brings greater fear, greater dread, to the human spirit than the thought of death? Throughout time, humankind had contrived scores of antidotes to its mortality. Ponce de Leon sought his Fountain of Youth. Others have sought magic cures, potions, and healers to extend their lives.

As the last glimmer of the afternoon sun slipped away, John Lee's eyelids moved. He'd been deep in a recurring dream of hunting the German tourist—a young and healthy lad he'd been—who'd tasted sweet. First, the thrill of the hunt. Second, the climax of the capture. Third, the wild plunge into satiation as he filled his senses with fresh blood.

But then came the nightmares. His fangs deep into a protruding vein, John Lee would hear the call of the priest amidst the shrieks of frenzied Indians—drums pounding, chants rising. The words would spill from the priest's lips like bile. He would look down at the lifeless limb he'd been holding, and for a brief moment, he would remember. He'd once been a stout fellow who'd laughed with friends, drank beer, sailed the high seas. Now he was just a savage. A lonely, hungry beast trapped by a curse that allowed no escape.

John Lee began to toss and turn. A low, bloodcurdling moan escaped from his lips.

His eyes blinked open, and he could immediately feel his heart slamming against his chest.

The waking was always the same. It was in that brief moment when torn away from his dreams that he would piece together the foggy components of his sleeping visions. It was in that small period of time that he'd be able to recall the fateful decision that had sealed his destiny, perpetuated his pain, stolen his freedom. And then, as quickly as it had returned, the memory would recede, and he would rise again to hunt.

He crawled out from his crevice and stood to face the night sky. The tip of the sun was the half-moon of a fingernail on the horizon, safe enough for him to emerge. His predator's eyes darted around the island. He licked his lips, and raised his nostrils to the night air in anticipation of his next meal. Where it would come from, he didn't know.

He stretched as he watched the sun bid its good-night. It was then he realized for the millionth time in three hundred years that he was tired. So, so tired.

The last sliver of the dying light reflected off a tear that ran down his face. So much pain. So much agony.

He raised his face to the sky and opened his

mouth, sending out a howl that pierced the night. Part of its volume was meant to raise his fellows, part of it was a vocalization of despair.

He began to move toward the beach, near the spit of land that connected the islands at low tide. It was there that he would wait for signs of life, life upon which he could feed.

He'd begun to sense that the three-hundred-year anniversary of the Feast of the Dead drew near. He sensed that somewhere far beyond his reach, lay his salvation. Beyond the farthest bounds of his vision lay one word, one word that could mean the end of his suffering: Mary.

He squatted on his haunches and opened his nostrils wide, waiting for food and deliverance.

CHAPTER 16

Searching

The holy man had been walking through the business district of Marathon for many hours. His feet hurt; his white jacket was too heavy under a merciless sun; he was tired.

He'd been scouring the area for several hours in search of further information from the locals surrounding the myth of the island he heard about from the women at church. His mission had taken on a whole new importance.

He hailed a cab and moved inside.

"Where to?" the black cabdriver asked.

Reverend Moses stared at the back of the driver's head as he pulled away from the curb.

"The question, my brother," Reverend Moses said in a cool voice, "is where do *you* want to go?"

He could see the bright whites of the driver's eyes in the rearview mirror.

"What?"

Placing his hand on the front seat, Reverend Moses leaned forward so that his mouth was inches from the driver's ear.

"I've traveled far and wide," the reverend continued, "and I've learned the smell of sin. I can smell it all over you."

Taking his eyes off the road, the driver turned

to look at the holy man. The reverend's assessment wasn't far off: It was the same cabdriver Tina had seen at the airport. The one she'd seen at Jeremy's meeting.

The driver pulled over to the curb.

"You can get out right here, mister."

"If you do not change your ways and accept salvation, you will go to Hell," the reverend replied, not moving an inch.

The driver now turned fully to face him.

"You're crazy, man. Get out of my cab."

Reverend Moses merely smiled. He'd been around: He'd been spat at, called names, assaulted. All are the price you pay when doing the Lord's work.

"I only want to help you," he said. "But first you must help yourself. Take me for a ten-dollar ride, and you may then drop me off when the meter's run out."

The driver looked longingly at the money. It had been a relatively slow day, and he had six dollars in his wallet. He was sure a ten-dollar ride would get him a tip.

"Fine," he said, snatching the ten. "But it don't mean I have to listen to your nonsense."

The cab pulled away from the curb.

"I know you believe in ghosts, my brother," the reverend continued. "But I want to tell you about another ghost, the Holy Ghost…"

And so the monologue began. In his search

to destroy the perpetrators of evil on the island, he needed to find its leader. He was confident that these same people would lead him to the island...and the undead.

The reverend knew that in time he would meet his archenemy and he would cast whatever it was back into the pit of darkness where it belonged.

Just a few miles away, Sheriff Amory Diggs pulled into Peter's Bait and Boat Shop. The proprietor, Hank Peters, had called again with a fresh gripe about the boat he'd reported missing.

He got out and entered the shop, sending several bells attached to the door jingling.

Hank Peters emerged from a room in the back. "Hello, Sheriff," the slumped-over, balding man said. He looked concerned.

"Howdy, Hank," the sheriff replied.

Sheriff Diggs had done a commendable job skirting the German consulate for the day. But now here was Hank Peters complaining about his lousy old boat again. The sheriff had indeed driven around for a few minutes during the last few weeks looking for it. But after checking out the lagoons and swamps while driving sixty-five down Highway One, he'd decided it was nowhere to be found. It would show up sooner or later, and he had better things to do.

His stomach grumbled as he thought of a

strawberry-frosted doughnut.

"Sheriff," Hank said, "you've got to find that boat. It's been three weeks now, and I've lost out on three week's rental. You know how much it'd cost me to get a new boat?"

"No, Hank, how much?"

"More than I got to spend," Hank replied. "You gotta keep lookin'."

"I'm right on top of it, Hank," Sheriff Diggs said as he turned to leave.

Turning up Jimmy Buffett on the radio in his car, Diggs leaned back and scratched his belly.

"Ah, life in the Keys," he said, and he began to laugh. "What a joke. You tell em' Jimmy. Got nothin' better to do than go lookin' for a miser's boat. That and a drunk German."

After spitting out the window, he turned out onto the road and sped away, content with the day's achievements.

CHAPTER 17

Vanished

As Mary stepped through the door of Tina's house, she was overwhelmed by the changes that jarred with her childhood memories.

"Where's Aunt Elly?" Mary asked, referring to Tina's mom.

Tina walked down the hallway toward the kitchen. "She's probably upstairs," she called back over her shoulder.

Mary could hear the kitchen faucet running as Tina filled a glass with water.

Unease sat inside her like a lump. She could tell that Tina was hiding something. She wasn't concerned only with Jeremy; there was surely something else.

The gloominess of the house gave her a good indication that something had changed in the Tipton household. The possibilities were end-less.

"Kind of dark in here, isn't it?" Mary asked as Tina came back down the hallway with the glass of water in her hand.

"Mom likes the curtains drawn," Tina replied, sipping from her glass.

"Well, I guess it does keep the house cooler in the summer," Mary said with the hope of adding something trivial to ease the tension.

Tina said nothing; she only looked at her cousin. The silence created a current of tension that was palpable.

"When's your dad coming back from Saudi Arabia?" Mary asked. She knew that her uncle worked for an oil company and that he'd been in the Middle East for several years. As far as she knew, he came home only on holidays and short weeks during the fall.

"He writes a lot, saying he looks forward to coming home...next time," Tina replied. Here was yet something else Mary didn't know. Tina should have guessed that the truths would come out. She hadn't thought about how to tell Mary.

"He wants me to come visit him, but it's such a long way off," she continued.

"It might be a neat trip," Mary replied, her eyes scanning the house.

The foyer and the whole house were dark. Even the chandelier over the staircase seemed subdued, with no light reflecting from its crystals.

Tina finished her water and set the glass on a table. "I'll go check on Mom and tell her you're here," she said. "I'll be just a minute."

Once Tina had disappeared upstairs, Mary inched forward into the formal dining room on her left.

She attempted to distinguish the obvious changes from the more subtle ones.

Odd! The dining room was prepared as though the Tiptons' were expecting special guests. The table was set with fine Irish linen and place settings for four. Even the water goblets were set out.

It's too perfect. It's like they had it set for Better Homes and Gardens *or something.*

Because the light coming into the house was so bleak, she could not distinguish much except the fine coat of dust covering everything.

It's as though no one's been in this room for years.

Her mind tried to ad-lib a reasonable explanation for the scenario. She deduced something to the effect that it'd been all laid out for Tina's father on some night in the recent past when he was expected home. He hadn't come home that night, and they had never cleared the table.

She turned to her right, crossing the hallway into the living room. It too was very dark, with the exception of a few flickering candles. The drapes and shutters were drawn tightly.

It's like they're trying to keep the daylight out.

Though the candlelight offered some light, the finer details of the room were hard to figure out. She was able to make out the bulky shapes of the old-fashioned furniture she remembered from a decade ago.

She moved farther into the room to get a better look at the other objects hiding in the darkness. Pictures and knickknacks struck faintly familiar chords as her mind raced to place them.

The candles threw dancing shadows on the walls. It was more than a bit odd, for though the sun was almost down, there was still enough twilight to illuminate a room. With the curtains open, one candle would have sufficed.

She gradually realized that there were pictures everywhere: albums, frames, loose ones, old ones, new ones.

There were hundreds of these photographs scattered throughout the room. Rummaging through one stack on a table in the corner, she uncovered the first of several mysteries contained within the Tipton home.

The stack she was holding was from a different time. But there was one constant: a little boy...a boy Mary had never seen before...one she'd never even heard Tina mention.

And yet there he was, laughing in Tina's father's arms, cuddling close to his mother, smiling as a gap-toothed youth can.

"It's a bit sad, isn't it?"

Tina's voice from behind made Mary drop the pictures and they scattered like confetti on the floor.

"Tina!" Mary shrieked. "Don't ever sneak up on me like that again!" Her heart was trying desperately to control its racing pulse.

"I'm sorry. I guess you didn't hear me come down the stairs."

Tina was standing at the doorway, hovering just outside the room.

"Is your mother coming down?" Mary said. She felt caught in the act of doing something terribly wrong.

Tina shrugged. "Mom's asleep right now, let's just put your stuff away."

Hesitant to ask but determined to do so, Mary swept her arms around the room. "What is it with all these pictures? And who's the little boy?"

Tina's eyes dropped for a moment, then rose to meet Mary's in a pain-filled gaze.

"That's Baby Eddie," she said in a flat, emotionless tone.

"Baby who?" Mary asked, turning to pick up a large silver-framed photo of the small boy holding a toy.

"Baby Eddie. He was Mom and Dad's first-born."

"Firstborn?" Mary coughed. She looked down at the picture in her hands. "How come I never knew about him?"

"I didn't know anything about him either until I turned twelve. That's when they told me about him."

"Told you about him?" Mary said in astonishment. "You mean you didn't know you had a brother?"

Tina shrugged. "What can I say?"

"What happened?" Mary pressed. "Did he die?"

Tina looked around the room and turned to leave, hoping Mary would follow. "Why don't we talk about it later? Are you thirsty?"

Mary decided she might as well press on. "Where is he then if he didn't die?" she asked.

"He died," Tina said, as if that was that. *Finis.*

"He died," Mary repeated to herself. "You had a brother, and he died. And your mother never told you until you were twelve, and she never told my mom or anything."

"Look," Tina said sternly. "Baby Eddie just died."

"And that's it?"

Tina's shoulders slumped. She looked defeated, older than her years. "No. It's worse than that."

"What then?" Mary asked, a morbid curiosity rising from beneath her desire to know the simple truth.

"Mom and Dad could have handled his just dying. At least then they would have known," Tina said wistfully.

"I don't understand," Mary said, really curious now.

Tina took a deep breath. "Mom and Dad

met just out of high school. Mom got pregnant, and she and Dad moved away from home here to the Keys. They were ashamed at first, so they never told anyone that she was pregnant. After Eddie was born, he was the center of their lives. Everything they did, they did for him. Then one day, a few years later, he disappeared."

"Disappeared?"

Tina nodded. "Stolen. One minute he was playing out back, the next minute he was gone."

"Oh, how sad. I'm sorry, Tina," Mary said with both shock and compassion.

"Yeah, it seemed sad when I heard it," Tina said, a rage at injustice trailing behind her words.

Mary's eyes dropped from Tina's, and she turned to look around the room once again.

Mary put a silver-framed photo down and picked up a smaller one in a wooden frame. "Poor Aunt Elly. It must have been terrible for her—not knowing for all of these years."

Tina looked up at her. "She's never given up hope. She keeps saying Eddie will walk in through that door one day."

Mary detected the hidden resentment in Tina's voice. "You don't believe that, do you?"

"Sure I do," Tina spat in an attempt to rebuke her doubts. "I believed it from the day I helped her set that dining room table for the formal dinner. The one we'll have when Eddie returns."

Mary looked toward the dining room.

"That's why the table's set like that? I thought it was for your father."

Tina shook her head. "Mom had a breakdown or something a few years ago. You should have seen her, running around, getting things nice and neat, because she thinks he's coming back."

"Is that when she told you about Eddie?"

"You mean *Baby* Eddie," Tina said, scolding her cousin for her incorrect address. "That's the way she refers to him," Tina continued. "Like he's in some time warp and will come through the door like the young boy he once was. Like time would stop for her so she could find the lost years."

Mary looked at Tina and waited until words could come. "I guess it's been hard on you, too."

A switch flicked on inside Tina and she opened up her heart to her sorrow. "Mom's become stranger every year. She keeps candles lit in vigilance, pictures displayed in the living room..."

Tina stepped into the room. She ran her fingers along the dust-covered tables, drawing an aimless pattern. "She keeps to herself in that upstairs sitting room," Tina said, nodding toward the stairs. "Just sits there in her rocker every day, reading her Bible. Over and over again."

"That's all she does?" Mary asked, thinking of

her aunt spending long hours in solitude.

"That's all. No cooking, no washing, nothing. Just reads the Bible and talks to herself."

Tina stopped and stared at a patchwork of photos. "It's been like being locked in a tomb with the dead. She doesn't talk about anything except a dead boy she thinks is coming back."

"What about your dad?" Mary asked. "What does he think?"

"Dad tried to talk with her, tried to get her counseling, but she won't go. They've drifted apart."

This was no holiday. Mary wished she had stayed home. But here she was in a strange room in a strange house. And upstairs lived a strange woman—her aunt—who kept a missing son alive in a pathetic memorial.

Tina continued. "Dad tried. He did. But he just couldn't take it anymore. The oil company offered him a lucrative job in Saudi Arabia, and he took it because he said we needed the money. But I think it was really to get away from Mom and this...this...insanity."

Mary wanted to hug her cousin, to comfort her for all she must have endured through the years.

Tina pulled the curtains apart letting in bright light that cut the darkness like a sharp blade. "All she does is wait for the day when Baby Eddie comes bouncing in with a smile on his face and a toy in his hand."

Her family's deepest, darkest secret was out, and Tina felt shame and hurt and sorrow.

Mary stepped forward and put a hand on Tina's shoulder. "It's okay. You don't have to talk about it anymore."

"You just don't understand!" Tina said through flowing tears. "My mom's not right! She's had a breakdown...She's crazy."

Trying to hid her anguish, Tina turned from Mary.

"Why did they wait so long to tell you?" Mary asked quietly.

Tina's voice came out in a whisper as she wiped tears from her face. "It happened before I was born, and they thought they could bury it in their memories. Mom didn't want another baby, but Dad thought that having one would help her forget Baby Eddie."

"So you came along," Mary said, filling in her cousin's story.

Tina nodded. "I came along...but I didn't do any good. Your family moving here helped her because she needed to hide the truth. But after you moved away, everything just fell apart."

Tina paused as a fresh wave of sobs racked her.

"Don't say anything more," Mary whispered, reaching out to hug her cousin.

Tina's body convulsed beneath Mary's embrace.

"She drove Dad away! I've got nothing and no one!"

"Oh, Tina!" Mary moaned. She hugged her close, wishing in that moment that she could absorb some of the pain that was too much for one person to bear alone.

The two girls cried together in the deepening shadows of the dark room.

CHAPTER 18

Waiting for Baby Eddie

Only up the stairs but a world away, Elly Tipton stared out the window and blinked as she watched the sun go down. She had heard the girls crying but thought it was little Eddie screeching with joy.

"Is that you, son?" she whispered, licking her chapped, dry lips.

But as the sobs quieted, no more could be heard from Eddie. She realized he had not yet come. She rubbed her fingers over the leather cover of the Bible on her lap.

"You'll be home soon, my little Eddie," she sighed.

Elly Tipton's head fell forward in a light sleep, her chin slumped down on her chest. Her glasses slipped down her nose. She made a soft snuffing sound as she breathed.

A soft breeze came in through the slightly opened window, rustling the Bible's pages, which lay open to Revelations, Chapter 13.

Descending once again into her dreams, she found herself in the same place she'd always been since Eddie had disappeared. A dream that had been dreamt a thousand times.

As she crossed over the familiar terrain, her mind raced, her lips occasionally mumbling the words she'd memorized from the Bible:

> *The beast will be worshipped by all those inhabitants of the earth who did not have their names written in at the world's beginning in the book of the living, which belongs to the Lamb who was slain...*

She saw Baby Eddie again. Saw him being ripped apart. "Eddie! Eddie!" she screamed in her sleep.

She awoke with a start and the Bible slipped to the floor. She leaned over and picked it up, rubbing her eyes.

Again it had seemed so real. The beast had been very close, and she could smell its foul stench.

"Dreaming again," she whispered. "Bad dream."

As her grip on wakefulness calmed her, she remembered the words of the chapter she'd been reading: "...which belongs to the lamb who was slain."

A tear dropped from her right eye.

In her dreams, the vision had come: A vision of that terrible moment when she thought she knew what had happened to her baby. It would never leave her alone. Not ever.

Elly blinked. *My little lamb was slain. My little Eddie.*

She had not always been as tormented as now.

At first she had tried to accept the pain of Eddie's disappearance and to suffer in silence as first the neighbors and then the police slowly adjusted to his absence, and ultimately moved on to other things.

She could not. She'd been able to hide the pain for a while, confident that her boy would reappear and return to her. And that hope alone is what she clung to in the early years like a rope tossed inches from a drowning swimmer.

Pain and guilt formed a cancer more malignant than any tumor. Even Tina's birth failed to ease the despair.

Elly knew what it was that had driven her husband away, what it was that had backed her into this corner where she was left with nothing but rage and a broken heart.

It was the tenth year after Eddie's disappearance when her mental health broke.

She'd been alone in the kitchen, her husband out of town on business. She'd been washing the dishes after dinner. Evening was coming on. The house was quiet.

She'd watched Eddie playing in the backyard through the window over the sink. It was the last place he had been seen alive.

It was then that everything had taken on an air of unreality. The backyard had started shimmering as if caught in the path of a tremendous heat wave. Little Eddie faced the window, waving, and calling to her frantically.

"Mama! Mama! Help me, Mama!"

"Oh, Lord," she moaned, gripping the countertop.

She'd closed her eyes and shook her head, as if that would clear it away.

No, she'd thought. *This can't be real.*

She opened her eyes again, and little Eddie was still standing on the grass, calling to her. *"Help me, Mama!"*

"Is that you, baby?" she'd whispered, her feet frozen in her place.

Suddenly the boy screamed, a terrible, blood-curdling scream.

"Eddie!" she'd shouted instinctively, forcing her feet to move.

In the vision she watched him—helpless, fragile, vulnerable, looking over his shoulder, horror on his face.

He screamed again. *"Help, Mama!"*

Her trembling hands had yanked open the door and she'd run out. Her feet couldn't move fast enough. What she thought she'd seen would change her life forever.

Little Eddie was caught in a circle of encroaching horrible monsters. Thick strings of saliva had dripped and hung from their fangs.

"Help me, Mama," he'd cried for the last time, his voice barely above a whisper. He'd started quietly sobbing as the monsters, creatures from

beyond the grave, closed in on him and started tearing him apart.

And still she was unable to move. Unable to help. It'd all been too fast, too unexpected, too horrible. Her mind was never the same.

His frightened, pleading eyes had remained locked on hers until the life left them.

And then the monsters disappeared, dragging Eddie with them.

"God help him," was all she'd been able to say, was all she could say now.

He was gone as though he'd never been.

A life stolen.

A life that Elly Tipton still clung to as she flicked off the lamp at her side, ready to fight the oncoming shadows and demons of the night.

CHAPTER 19

Lost Boat

A mile from Peters Bait and Boat Shop, Sheriff Diggs slammed on the brakes. "Forgot to get me a soda," he said. It was almost the end of the day, which meant the end of his shift. There wasn't much else to do, and he was darned thirsty.

He turned around and drove back to the shop. Opening the door, he set off the bells again. He walked across the shop to the cooler and snatched an ice-cold Mountain Dew. Hank Peters wandered out from the back.

"Back so soon, Sheriff?" he said, wiping his hands on his jeans.

Embarrassed that he'd returned only for a soda, Diggs took immediately to questioning. Of course he'd heard it all before, but it was still hot outside and the soda tasted mighty good. He settled in and listened to Peters' blather while enjoying the coolness of the beverage.

Soon he'd be faced with a stream of verbal garbage from the parents of snot-nosed kids on Midsummer's Eve and the kids themselves. It was always a tough night...hard work. Midsummer's Eve was all fun and games to the kids, but to him it was a night when he had his hands full.

Diggs couldn't remember a single Midsummer's Eve since joining the force when he didn't have at least half the jail cells filled.

Normally, his on-the-job hours were spent avoiding trouble and paperwork, with a specialization in passing the buck wherever and whenever he could. And eating lots of doughnuts.

Though his habits resulted in backed-up cases and few convictions, his live-and-let-live philosophy found favor with many of the locals. He had a way of closing his eyes to the petty stuff everyday people did to survive, and that suited a lot of them just fine.

"So the tourist just took your boat and didn't bring it back? That's it?"

"Like I told ya, Sheriff," Peters replied. "I just want my boat back. Aside from the money lost in rentals, I've got an investment in those things. Bought each of them boats with my own hard-earned cash. Ain't got no insurance, neither."

"Anything else?" Diggs asked, praying he wouldn't have to listen to Peters' story a third time. He was happy he'd had the soda, but he questioned the price of hearing it again.

"Just keep your ears open for any mention of his name," Peters replied.

"What was his name again? I know it was in the papers."

Peters held up his boat-rental ledger. "Name's Hans Schultz."

"Okay," Diggs relied, grabbing another can of soda fro the road. "I'll be on the lookout for Hans Schultz and arrest him when I find him."

To Diggs' surprise, Peters shook his head. "I think you ain't gonna do spit," he said. "You just be talkin' through your tail with a full wind behind you."

"What do you want me to do? I told ya I got priorities. I'll look around, but that's about all I can do."

"Can't be that many Germans runnin' around here right now. Heck, the guy couldn't hardly speak English."

Sheriff Diggs pulled out a little pad of paper and began to scribble some pertinent information, such as the description of the small skiff and the local hotel information that was on the rental slip. Of course it was all procedure to be followed on the first call, but that was a whole different story.

As Diggs opened another soda and got a bag of chips, the irritating bell over the front door jingled. The pilot from USAir entered, searching for fishing supplies.

"How are the fish bitin'?" he said to the two men.

Diggs shrugged, but Peters grinned, which was part of his job. Grin, tell fish stories, and sell bait and beer.

"Heard they're bringin' in big ones just south

of here," he said to the customer.

"How about 'round the lagoon?" the captain asked, hoping he wasn't being too specific in case he might give away his secret place.

"You mean the one over by the tide island?" Peters asked, referring to Vampire Island.

Since it was only accessible during low tides, Peters and the other local fishermen used a more realistic name for the place. Or so they thought.

"Yeah, in that area," the captain replied, still hoping that there were other lagoons in the same vicinity to which they might be referring. He gathered his items and put them on the counter.

"I'm told it's fine," Peters said, ringing up the items on his cash register.

"I gotta go," Sheriff Diggs said, his hands now full with soda and chips.

"Just find my boat, will ya?" Peters said as the fat man opened the door.

"I'll do my best," Diggs replied. "Let me know if you think of anything else."

For the second time in less than an hour, Diggs pulled away from the store. The first thing he did as he turned onto the main road was radio the Coast Guard, to whom he passed the buck. Let them worry about the lost boat and tourist for at least that evening.

The good old pass the buck. Diggs' effective standard method of operation.

Which was why the only ones sniffing around

for Hans Schultz were the animals and insects of the lagoon. After all, the scent of blood is hard to erase. A lot harder than the body itself.

Poor Hans; he'd come a long way from Berlin to die. A long, long way.

But things of all varieties happened in the Keys. One could have the time of his life or lose his life. It all went with the territory.

Especially when that territory was Vampire Island.

CHAPTER 20

Nosy Neighbors

Mrs. Martin continued to stare out her side window at the Tipton's house. She'd seen the two girls arrive.

"Sam?" she said to her husband with her face still plastered to the glass. "Sam, they got a visitor next door."

"'Bout time," he replied, putting his paper down. His cigar was burnt almost to the filter. "Now you mind your business and quit peepin' on other folks."

"It's a young girl," she said, ignoring his request. "Tina's friend or something."

"I know what you might be thinkin', woman, but it ain't your business."

Mrs. Martin shook her head. "I'll bet she doesn't know Tina's mom's nuts."

"If she don't," he said, rustling the paper as he opened it to the sports page, "then who cares? Why do you?"

She shook her head again and bit her lip. Her mind traveled back to that day when the neighborhood had first realized that Mrs. Tipton had gone mad.

She had been in her own yard hanging clothes, in between the rows of white sheets flapping in the summer breeze, when Elly Tipton had come running out of her house screaming.

Mrs. Martin broke from her thoughts and coughed. "Not right havin' neighbors like that," she said, frowning. She turned to look at her husband. "If you ask me, that Tipton woman should be put away. That young girl shouldn't be stayin' there."

"How do you know she's stayin' there?" her husband replied from behind the screen of his newspaper. "How do you know anythin', woman?"

"'Cause I saw 'em carry in a suitcase," she replied. *So there, Mr. Smartypants.*

Mrs. Martin turned to the window again. "I'll bet she's here for that teen wingding comin' up."

Like most adults in the Keys, she regarded Midsummer's Eve with no small degree of apprehension. It was a night to stay home and lock the doors.

Opening the curtains wider, she said, "The question is, does that girl know how crazy that woman is?"

When her husband didn't answer, she closed her mouth.

God protect her precious soul.

CHAPTER 21

Evil Presence

In her room in the Tipton house, Elly's mind continued to replay her dark vision.

The memories would come and come again, and she'd learned long ago that no matter how hard she tried to tell others of what had happened that day, no one would believe her.

She sobbed. "I'm not crazy," she whispered, flipping her Bible to Revelations, Chapter 22, where she kept a photograph of her son.

With shaking fingers she took the photo and kissed it, wetting it with her tears. She moaned her boy's name. "Oh, Eddie, Eddie, Eddie," she softly whimpered.

"God give me strength," she whispered.

Elly focused on the open page of the Bible that rested on her lap, and she read aloud to herself from Verse 11:

> *Let the wicked continue in their wicked ways, the depraved in their depravity! The virtuous must live on in their virtue and the holy ones in their holiness.*
>
> *Remember I am coming soon!*

Then she heard something. "Who's there?" Elly called out, startled.

She heard her niece's voice downstairs. Where before she'd heard them crying, she now heard them laughing, a sound that hadn't been heard in her house in years.

She vaguely remembered Tina coming in, saying that Mary had arrived.

Tina's laughter could be heard in turn, and she smiled, "It's been a long time," she said, nodding her head. She began to slowly rock in her chair.

Elly had not been happy with the idea of her sister's daughter coming to visit, but she still had enough goodwill left in her to recognize that it might be good for Tina. The idea of Midsummer's Eve hadn't entered her thoughts, since she was unaware that Tina had snuck out to attend it the year before.

There were many moments when Elly knew that her watch for Eddie was hard on Tina. Those moments more than anything else made her regret the way her life had impacted her family.

There had even been weak moments when the weight of the words in her Bible seemed to make the struggle unbearable. When giving up and moving away in search of a different life seemed the easiest way out.

To forget Baby Eddie. To forget what she saw. To forget the evil.

At certain times, it seemed like the right thing to do.

But she knew in her heart that the vision

would follow her wherever she went.

Now she heard another voice, and she was sure it didn't belong to either of the two girls downstairs.

"What?" she mumbled, looking around.

A silence hung heavy in the air.

After a few moments, the voice whispered to her. It definitely was not either of the girls.

"Who is it?" Elly asked, whipping her head around. "Show yourself," she commanded, suddenly afraid not only for herself.

The voice—low, deep, and hard to decipher—caused her to strain her ears. She soon began to believe that it was coming from somewhere inside her head.

Lord, what is this I'm hearing?

Her temporary courage was fading rapidly.

The voice laughed.

Her wide eyes scanned the room.

It's evil. It's the beast. It's the presence and it's come to find me.

Not knowing what else to do she began to pray.

"The Lord is my shepherd; I shall not want."

Elly Tipton prayed with a passion born of fear. To ward off the presence that had entered the house to torment her.

It seemed very close. Possibly as close as the next room or the front porch. Was she truly mad? Or was she just imagining things?

"Show yourself," she commanded again, trying to keep her breath to a slow, measured pace.

But nothing came. Nothing moved.

There was just the voice and her beating heart.

"Show yourself if you dare, in the name of the Lord."

The curtains stayed almost shut, and the door didn't move.

Her thoughts, scrambled in fear, began manipulating a line she'd read only moments ago.

Remember, I am coming soon.

Who—what—was coming soon? The beast was coming soon!

A chill crept up her legs.

Again, from somewhere unknown, a deep, dark, guttural voice snarled at her, playing on her disorientation.

Remember, Elly. I am coming soon. I'm everywhere, right behind you.

"Damn you!" she yelled. "Show yourself!"

She could feel a stirring in the air mirrored by the revived stirring of the wind coming in through the window.

It was him—or them—whatever had taken her baby. They were somewhere near enough to be felt. Somewhere as close as...

Sawgrass Key?

She didn't know why that name suddenly

popped into her head, but it did.

That name set off a flurry of images that reaffirmed all the reasons she'd never left. Eddie needed a place close by to which he could return. He was not far. He might even be as near as...

Sawgrass Key.

The name pulled at her from opposing directions. It created feelings of warmth, of love, of Eddie. It created feelings of hate, of monsters, of Evil.

Pulling her shawl around her neck, Elly Tipton could feel the presence gain strength. It was coming alive on the island as darkness descended, just as it had for three hundred years. The evil was the vampires.

Was there evil inside her home? She wasn't sure.

But it certainly wasn't far away.

Of that, she was sure.

CHAPTER 22

The Awakening

Slowly, the other vampires on the island stirred awake. They'd heard the calling of their leader; and the darkness, as it had done for three hundred years, bid them welcome.

Like John Lee, they often tired of their existence. For three hundred years they had endured an endless cycle of death and rebirth: dying before dawn and beginning their grueling resurrection in the shadows of the twilight hours.

And this they had done day after day after day. It was a life not worth living.

They were not aware that Sheriff Diggs had called the Coast Guard to continue the search for the missing tourist, but they had no need to fear intrusion. What remained of the German after they had feasted was long gone with the tide, the odd remaining bits and pieces fought over by the fish.

There was the boat. The Coast Guard might find the boat. But what good was the boat without the human life that had occupied it? The boat could be washed, repaired, and returned. It was the murder of a man that could bring the wrath of the living down upon them and their island.

The living thought the waters surrounding

the southern tip of the state were shark-filled. If search parties had not found a missing boater within several days, they would often write it off as a casualty of the treacherous waters of the Gulf Stream. Hans Schultz was just another casualty.

Food was becoming a luxury. There had been a time when they'd been able to draw wayward ships in to land by using the trickery of their lights. But modern navigation instruments had made large feasts of hapless crews a thing of the past.

How they longed for the past, when ships carrying as many as thirty or forty sailors dropped anchor off the shore of the island. How they'd taken for granted the wild feasts.

Now they were lucky to get a small fishing boat with one fisherman once every cycle of the moon. Even when they were fortunate enough to see sustenance, the meal would often fail to come ashore.

Modern technology wasn't their only opponent. The lone fisherman who saw the vampires swinging their lights to draw him in often mistook them for drug dealers signaling for unseen boats in dark waters.

The only gift that darkness brought was the occasional tourist like Hans. Finding Hans had been sheer luck.

They were forced to wait for someone to

make a mistake. A very fatal mistake.

The other vampires gathered and found John Lee. Standing on the edge of the lagoon, the vampires scanned the water's horizon, praying to whatever dark force guided them for a boat with people.

Off in another direction, they saw the lights of Marathon reflected in the night sky, but they'd learned some time ago the dangers of moving too far inland.

There had been times in the past when they'd acquired food by raiding small shanties. The very last time they'd been able to feed deep into Marathon was when they'd taken a small boy almost twenty years before.

Even that last experience had proven dangerous. Desperate for blood, searching for vulnerable prey, they'd become lost. They'd finally spotted a boy alone in a yard—had jumped him without hesitation—but a woman had seen them and run out screaming.

The woman's having seen them was dangerous. They may have been reduced to savages, but they still had the survival instinct. The woman could round up others who would surely come to destroy them.

So they'd retired the last two decades to feeding on whatever came near or on the island. Not a single opportunity was wasted. Food had become a precious commodity.

Suddenly they saw lights approaching across Sawgrass Key. Someone had stepped within their bounds.

Their eyes flickered. Their hearts pounded. Their tongues hung from their mouths.

They began to fidget with excitement. Car lights meant only one thing to them: Life. Life with blood in it that could sustain them until their next feeding. And as experience had taught them, those meals were few and far between.

The tide was low, and darkness had worked its magic. As the car's lights went out and they heard the sound of a car door slamming, the scent of fresh blood pumping through someone's veins gained intensity.

They wished at that moment more than ever that something could cure their plight, and the painful drought of abundant, life-preserving food. If only they could feed again like they had in days of old.

They were so, so hungry.

Picking up their lights, they began their slow tread toward the smell. Each of the six creatures had only one thought in mind.

They were going to find out who had come to dinner.

CHAPTER 23

Foul Demon

Tina had finally overcome her distress, and
the two girls had ended the episode in the living
room laughing with each other. After the tension broke they had both succumbed the only
way they knew how: They became giddy.

In better spirits, Tina prepared a light dinner
for them. She'd thought her mother might like
to come and join them, but when she went up to
ask, she found her even more withdrawn than
earlier.

"But Mary's here, Mom. You really should
come down and…"

Elly Tipton waved her silent. "She's not welcome here."

Tina was doubting her listening skills.
"What?"

"Send her home."

"But, Mom!" Her forehead wrinkled up.
"She just got here!"

Elly Tipton shook her head. "Home. Send
her home. I don't want her kind here."

Tina felt like screaming. First, she had had to
grapple with the whole issue of Jeremy and his
questionable interests. Then she had had to
scuffle with Mary's response. Now it was her
mother.

At that moment she could still pity her mother's grief, but understanding had its limits. There was a time to mourn and a time to relax. Baby Eddie was gone—had been for a long time—and she'd had her share of mourning. Enough was enough.

When is this going to stop? she wondered.

Never, she answered herself. *It will go on and on.* She sighed, shaking her head.

"Get her out, Tina," Elly said looking away.

Tina tried another approach.

"Why don't you just come down and have some salad with us?" she said. "You need to have something to eat. You're thin as a rail."

"I won't eat with her."

Suddenly furious, Tina boldly stepped forward, her eyes blazing, and grabbed her mother's hand.

"Stop it!" she yelled into her mother's face. She wanted to shake her, wake her from this insanity.

"You don't understand," her mother mumbled, resisting her daughter's grasp.

Tina let go and stepped back. "I *don't* understand," she said. "Mary is family. I invited her to stay with us, and you said okay."

Her mother looked sternly ahead out the window to something only she could see. "That was before I knew."

"Knew what? Is there something wrong?

Gosh, Mom," she said, her voice softer. "You haven't even said hi to your own niece."

Her mother continued to stare, unchanged.

"Very well, then," Tina said. She turned and stopped at the doorway. "We'll eat by ourselves. I'll just tell her you're not feeling well. But I will bring her up, Mother, and you will be kind to her."

The two girls enjoyed a light dinner of Caesar salad and garlic breadsticks. As they finished eating, Tina thought of her mother. She considered not taking Mary up there until the next day; perhaps her mother would then be in somewhat better spirits. But Mary kept asking about her, wondering about her, until Tina knew that it needed to be done and over with.

They cleared the table and walked to the foot of the stairs.

"Let's make this quick," Tina said nervously. "Mom's been pretty down lately."

Mary nodded. "I just want to say hello."

Mary had long since put the strange boy and the voice out of her thoughts. All she could feel at the moment was pity—pity for her aunt and for her cousin.

Tina could see the sincerity in Mary's eyes. Seeing it made her feel even worse. "I'm sorry," she said. "I guess the whole situation doesn't make this a very pleasant place to be."

Tina led the way up the darkness of the stairs.

"Watch your step," she said. "Mom doesn't like a lot of lights on." Then, making an excuse, "Saves electricity that way."

Mary tried to be cheerful. Things didn't have to be bad. She would put all this behind her and try to make her aunt feel like she'd truly been missed.

But the stairs and the second-floor hallway were as bad as the living room.

Though there were no candles or walls covered with pictures of Baby Eddie, there was the same oppressive sense of doom, a sense of foreboding that filled the air.

Tina knocked. Then opened the door and waited, looking hesitantly as if she were a stranger.

"Mom, Mary's here."

Silence.

"Mom," Tina said, her voice more stern, "Mary wants to say hello."

Tina still received no response. She turned and motioned for Mary to enter.

Mary stepped into the room behind Tina. She wasn't prepared for what she saw.

Recalling the memories of her youth, she remembered Aunt Elly as she had been: an attractive woman.

Here was a woman who looked twice her age. A woman with lost, hollow eyes who looked completely alien to Mary.

Mary tried to keep the shock from her face. She cleared her throat. "It—it's nice to see you again. How are you, Aunt Elly?"

Elly spun her head to look at Mary.

She could feel it. It was here. It was in her house and it was bad.

"Tina said you haven't been feeling very well," Mary said. Her aunt's stare froze Mary's thoughts.

"I'm fine," Elly replied, preparing to ward off the intruder. "I'm strong enough to fight you."

Tina knew her mother was losing it and took Mary by the arm.

"You here long?" Elly asked.

Mary wasn't exactly sure what the question meant. If it meant how long was she staying, it didn't make sense because Elly should already know. Was she suggesting Mary leave soon? She was beginning to think her aunt didn't recognize her. "Two weeks. If that's okay?"

"It's not long enough, is it, Mother?" Tina said, trying to command her mother with her eyes.

"If you say so," Elly said.

The evil was checking her out, getting a feel for her. If no one else knew it, she did.

She picked up the Bible, glaring at Mary. "Don't forget your prayers. Pray for the wicked to be cast into hell. Pray for the angels to watch over you. Pray for the blood of our Savior to be your salvation. You girls must pray."

Mary, distraught, looked to Tina for guidance.

Tina and Mary said goodnight and turned to go downstairs.

The evil was turning its back on Elly: It was vulnerable. She jumped up from her rocker, knocking it over, Bible held high above her head.

Tina turned. "Sit down, Mother."

Mary stepped forward.

"Foul demon!"

Mary couldn't believe her eyes or ears. "Excuse me?" she said.

Aunt Elly's eyes were ablaze.

"Begone, foul demon! You will not take another child from me!"

Tina's eyes brimmed with tears. "Come on, Mary. I told you Mom's not right."

Mary was speechless. Her aunt's hatred pierced through her.

Their eyes locked. For one brief moment, Tina was not in the room. No one lived in the world but the two of them.

"Aunt Elly," Mary stammered, wobbling on her feet.

Tina was yanking her cousin's arm. "Let's go. Now!"

Elly saw them begin to leave and dropped to her knees. "Our Father, who art in Heaven, hallowed be Thy name..."

Mary stared in horror.

"Come on, Mary!" Tina pulled Mary out into the hallway and slammed the door shut.

As they walked away, Mary could hear the words trailing after her down the stairs:

"Yea though I walk through the valley of the shadow of death...."

Outside on the sidewalk, a lone figure stood under the streetlight. Reverend Moses looked up to the window from which he'd heard the wailing.

At the reverend's urging, the cabdriver had dropped him off at a random street corner after his ten dollars had run out. He'd been walking for some time when Elly's words had pierced the darkness, stopping him dead in his tracks.

Listening to her words, he had felt her pain. He had known that she had seen the darkness, that she had met the beast.

Listening, he knew he was getting closer.

Monsters had taken her child. He needed to talk to her and hear her story.

She would lead him to them.

He knelt down on the sidewalk and began to pray.

CHAPTER 24

Night Creatures

The USAir captain slouched in his fold-up chair, rod firmly secured between his legs, his cooler at arm's reach. He looked up as a pelican flew over the calm water of his spot.

"Ahhhh," he sighed, raising a bottle of Heineken to his mouth. He drank greedily.

Though the thick darkness of the night should have driven him away long before, the captain relished the solitude. The day's routine was but a memory.

There was one problem with his special place, however—one he'd overlooked in his anticipation. Nighttime invited bugs of all sorts, and there wasn't enough bug spray in production to keep them away.

"Ouch!" he spat, slapping a mosquito on his neck.

Calculating the darkening hours, he debated how much longer he should stay. It was probably time to start packing the gear and getting out.

"No wonder they call this place Vampire Island," he said as he gathered his gear while fighting off insects. "Filled with darn bloodsuckers."

A slight movement seen from the corner of

his eye startled him; he'd been sure he was alone. The sudden idea of unknowingly sharing the same place with someone else disturbed him.

The movement continued, and he placed his belongings at his feet.

"What the hell?"

He pushed through the scrub to another lagoon. His heart skipped a beat as he laid eyes on a boat.

It was upside down, drifting toward land, fighting to stay above water.

"Is that the same one…?" He cut himself off.

Closer inspection revealed a bloody handprint on the boat's side. It was a print smeared down the side immediately causing the captain to believe that someone had dragged a hand, screaming until it fell.

"Oh jeepers," he said, running a hand through his hair. "I gotta report this."

His eyes darted around nervously. They stopped when they caught something flashing just across the lagoon.

Yes! Help was here!

He'd been afraid he was going to have to drive all the way back to Marathon to notify the police.

The lights bobbed up and down, back and forth, in the distance.

The captain ran back to his gear and swooped it up. When he returned to the edge of the lagoon, the lights had drawn nearer.

He suddenly felt a strange chill. Whomever held the lights moved them in a pattern, not like average people signaling or walking with a beam to guide their way.

"Hello! Hey!" he yelled in the lights' direction.

No one answered.

"Hey!"

He watched as they continued marching toward the lagoon. Their steady pace and silence entranced him, rousing his curiosity.

When they were but a small distance away a wave of oppressive air hit him followed by a putrid smell.

The lights continued to flicker and sway. The night sounds of an island became suddenly silent.

"Hey!"

When the shapes holding the lights again did not answer, his purpose changed. He was not going to talk to them or lead them to the mysterious boat. He was going to flee...fast.

The smell had him gagging by the time he reached his Toyota Land Cruiser. A headlamp cruising down the highway caught his attention, but he had no time to flag it down; in order to get to his secret spot, he'd pulled well away from the road.

He recklessly threw his gear into the backseat

of the Cruiser. Furiously fumbling in his pocket, he found the keys, and tried to start his car. His eyes glanced back to the direction of the lights.

He saw them for just a second before they disappeared, then heard a long, drawn-out sigh. The sound came from where he'd just been fishing.

The lights reappeared.

"Hello?"

The shapes holding them said nothing.

The lights, now only a short distance from the Cruiser, shifted their slow pattern, and one by one they were extinguished.

"What the...?" The captain squinted his eyes. "Where'd they go?"

For a moment he recalled *Miami Herald* headlines about hideous mutilations attributed to Colombian drug dealers. Perhaps he had stumbled upon one of their exchanges.

The stench returned even stronger.

It was coming from all directions. Through tearing eyes he saw what gave off the smell.

At first they were in front of the car, then they were moving around to its sides. Some went to the rear.

The captain gulped, feeling dizzy. He could have left gravel spraying behind spinning tires, but instead he had stayed, frozen yet fascinated.

A wave of communication spread among the creatures. They loomed—dark, disgusting, stinking—before and around him.

"What are you?" he asked.

They pressed forward.

"No! Get back!"

Arms extended, fangs bared, they converged on him.

"Oh no! Nooooo!" the captain screamed to a deaf world. The vampires dragged him from the car. There was nowhere to turn and no way out.

They howled, pinning him against the door. He struggled to break free. A long, agonizing shriek rose from him as a dozen points of pain pierced his body.

"Please! No!"

Teeth and fingers tore his flesh, the pain unlike anything he'd ever known or would know again.

His clothes torn free, his body became a carcass into which his hunters sank their teeth. He flailed, and he prayed, and he cried. Succumbing to their appetite, he slid lifelessly down to the gravel. His hand, like Hans', trailed lines of blood down the door.

The vampires gorged themselves in their wild gluttony. When they were done, what was left of the captain was an insult to the man he once was.

Like the unfortunate German, he'd strayed too close to a place where hunger knew no bounds.

Taking with them some remains for later, the vampires stumbled toward their home, gurgling and murmuring their satiation.

They waited for some time for the low tide, and after they had crossed, John Lee and two others hung back. The leader and his comrades were full, but they knew hunger would soon return.

They squatted near the spit of land that separated the islands. After some time, to their unexpected delight, they saw the parking lights of another car, stranded across the way on Highway One.

Darkness had brought them yet another victim.

They made their way toward the lights, eager to gather more food for the hours that certainly would have been spent in starvation.

The hapless tourist with car trouble couldn't possibly have any idea what awaited him. The only things his mind could focus on were his frustration and the spooky sounds of the night on the lonely stretch of road.

As quiet returned to the land near the lagoon, the island's other inhabitants emerged from their places of hiding, ready to feast on what the vampires had left behind. Crabs, sand beetles, and all the rest battled over what remained.

A USAir flight passed overhead, unaware that beneath it lay one of its best.

CHAPTER 25

Gossip

"Mary, I'm so sorry," Tina said as they reached the bottom of the stairs. "I told you," she whispered. "She's just not right."

The experiences of Tina's life formed a complex web of pain and Mary felt like she had walked into it. Mary reached out and touched Tina's arm. "You don't have to talk about it," she said.

Tina raised her eyes, took a deep breath, and tried to laugh. "Bet you weren't expecting all this, were you? Some vacation."

"You said she wasn't feeling well, but I didn't know what to expect," Mary replied. The experience with her aunt still had her quite shaken.

"Hey, come on," Tina said, forcing a smile. "We'll make this the best visit ever, right?"

"Right," Mary responded. She would do anything she could to lighten her cousin's load. She too pulled the corners of her mouth up into a smile.

"So let's do it."

Tina went to the refrigerator and pulled out a Jell-O pudding snack. "Want one?" she asked.

"No thanks."

Tina smiled. "Tell you what. Let's sit up and tell each other every little secret, with all the juicy details, what do you say?"

They perched themselves at the kitchen table. Tina told Mary of last year's Fourth of July date, when fireworks had exploded and she'd run with a wild group on Midsummer's Eve.

At Mary's turn, Tina asked, "What did you do with the ring after you and Keith called it off?"

"I sent it to him by mail with postage due," Mary said. "If he wanted it back badly enough, I decided he could pay to get it."

The two girls giggled, and the giggling felt good, so good. For the time being, the dark clouds hanging over their heads parted and they were just teenagers again.

They chatted the night away, moving from secret to secret, asking and telling things they would share with no other.

"Okay," Mary said some time after. "Now it's time to get some more details about the present."

"Okay," Tina said, nodding. "What about?"

"I want to hear more about the weird stuff you mentioned in the car today. You know, the occult stuff."

"Oh. That." Tina shrugged her shoulders. "I've just been messing around with some kids who like heavy metal. That's it."

"That's not how you put it in the car."

Tina had already told her about Jeremy and the strange things that went on throughout the island. It was time to let her cousin in on the reasons why she'd taken part.

Her voice took on a pained, serious tone. "Well, at first it was just to be with Jeremy. But then I started to realize that I'd also been looking for a way to make Mom better. I've prayed, and I've talked to God, and I've tried to talk with her. I've even pleaded with her to get professional help. When nothing seemed to work, I started looking anywhere I might find an answer."

"But Satanism?" Mary asked.

Tina sensed an attack. "So?"

"You really think Satan is a way to help your mom?" Mary asked.

"Well, they don't sacrifice anything," Tina replied, as though that would reduce the idea's strangeness.

Now Tina wished more than ever that she had been silent about it. She wished she could go back in time and refuse Jeremy's initial invitation to go out. Her heart beat restlessly for this wild boy who'd captured her fancy, but she still couldn't help wishing he'd never entered her life.

"What do you get out of going to the ceremonies?" Mary asked, interrupting Tina's thoughts.

Tina went on. "The first time they just chanted. I go because Jeremy wants me to."

"He must be very special to you."

Tina, half to herself, half to Mary, "Sometimes I wonder why I bother with him."

"You know, I'd kind of like to go to one of the ceremonies with you."

"Why?" Tina thought her cousin had already cast judgment. "I don't see you as one who would dabble in the occult."

"I didn't say I'd dabble. I'm just curious, that's all."

"No way," Tina said, shaking her head. "Nothing doing."

"C'mon, Tina!" Mary urged. "What would be the big deal if I watched?"

Tina looked at her cousin and all the arguments came back. She didn't want to place her in harm's way, but she also didn't want to alienate herself from Jeremy. He was weird, and he scared her sometimes, but she still had feelings for him.

Perhaps if she just took her for a few minutes and then left? That way both Jeremy *and* Mary would be satisfied. She would have lived up to her commitment to Jeremy and Mary could satisfy her curiosity.

Less than a minute later, Tina said, "Perhaps. But if we do, we'll stay on only one condition."

"What's that?" Mary said, feeling a strange exhilaration.

"We'll go, but if I tell you to leave, then you leave without question." The thought of Jeremy or anyone else frightening her cousin sent a shiver up her spine.

"Why?"

"Just because." What was she going to do about all of it: Jeremy, Mary, the meetings. She was confused.

After a moment of silence, Mary agreed, "Okay. Deal."

Tina placed her hand over Mary's. "It's just that I wouldn't want anything to happen to you."

Mary completely missed the implications of Tina's words. She'd figured the worst that could happen was her being kicked out of the meeting as an unwelcome stranger.

"What do I wear?" she asked eagerly.

"Don't worry. When the time comes, I'll pick something out for you."

The long day began to weigh heavily on Tina. She stretched and yawned. It was almost eleven-thirty.

"You tired?" Mary asked.

"It's been a long day. Let's get to bed. We need all the rest we can get for Midsummer's Eve."

And Jeremy's party.

They put their glasses in the sink and made for the stairs, turning out the kitchen light behind them.

Halfway up, Mary asked in the darkness, "Do they just do the devil stuff at night?"

"No. That's just in the movies. These heavy-metal types do things whenever they get the chance. You know, when their parents aren't watching."

"Then why are we going at night?"

"Shhh," Tina said, holding her index finger to her mouth. "Don't disturb Mother." Quietly, she continued. "Because that's when the party is. And that's when Jeremy wants you to come."

Mary stopped climbing. "He does?"

Tina turned. "Yeah. I told him you were coming to visit, and he said he wanted you to come to the meeting."

They reached the top of the stairs, carefully tiptoeing past Elly's room. When they arrived at the end of the hall at Tina's bedroom, Tina used the bathroom first, giving Mary a chance to put away her things.

Unpacking her suitcase, Mary fought back a creepy feeling that came from knowing her aunt was just down the hall probably thinking of a way to kill her. It took all she had to calm her nerves.

Tina finished in the bathroom, and it was Mary's turn to get ready for bed. Done within minutes, she returned, and Tina turned out the lights. Mary crawled into the cot that had been prepared for her.

The darkness of the room settled over them, and they remained quiet for some time, listening only to the sounds of the wind and the ticking clock.

Staring at the ceiling, Mary decided it was time to tell Tina about the voice.

"It was so real," she said. "Have you ever heard it, Tina?"

"You've got to be kidding," Tina laughed.

"I'm serious," Mary replied. "I heard it in my head, loud and clear. Right here." She tapped her temple with her index finger. "It's no joke."

When Tina failed to respond, Mary spoke. "Come on. I'll bet you know what I'm talking about." Taking into account all Tina had admitted about the occult, she wondered if Tina knew *exactly* what she was talking about.

Tina leaned up in her bed, looking across the room at Mary. "Yeah. Right."

"What do you think that was today? The voice, I mean. Does it have anything to do with Jeremy?"

Tina plopped back down on her bed. "Jeremy has a way about him. Let's leave it at that."

Mary could feel her heart thudding in her chest. "I wish it were as easy as that. It scared me, Tina."

Tina rolled over so that her back was to her cousin. "Go to sleep," she said to the wall. "You'll feel better tomorrow."

Oh, Jeremy. What have you done to my life?

"You're probably right," Mary said, pulling the covers up to her chin. "Good night."

"Sleep tight." Tina replied."

After a minute of silence, Mary spoke out softly. "Love you, Tina."

Tina fought back a tear. "Love you too, Mary."

Tina waited until she could hear the soft breath of Mary's sleep. She quietly pushed the covers down, grabbed a jacket. Stopping to look at the peaceful shape of Mary's body under the blanket, Tina then left the room and snuck out of the house, responding to the call of her heart.

It was almost midnight. Jeremy would be waiting.

CHAPTER 26

911

As soon as Sheriff Diggs stepped into the station to check his desk before retiring for the evening, a phone was shoved in his face.

"Now what?" he snarled, grabbing the phone from the dispatcher's hand. "Diggs here," he said into the mouthpiece.

His stomach grumbled and as he listened to the hysterical call. It was yet more tourist trouble; this time a man had stopped to check his engine just north of Maxi's Beer Corral and claimed to have seen vampires.

The tourist, his voice shaking, flew through the story at warp speed.

"Hold it! Hold it!" the sheriff shouted into the phone. The caller stopped in mid-sentence, falling completely silent. "Get ahold of yourself, boy! Have you been drinking?"

The tourist was bewildered. He was reporting a vampire sighting! "Uh, yeah. I had a couple."

"Uh-huh. A couple or a *couple*?"

"I had three drinks. That's all." Then, sensing what the sheriff was driving at, "I wasn't drunk, if that's what you're asking."

Sheriff Diggs nodded. *Yeah, right, pal.* "Why don't you meet me here at the station so we can talk about this, okay?"

No way, the tourist thought.

He hung up the phone.

"What a waste," he said as he stepped out of the booth. "Why'd I even call?"

He knew the creatures he'd seen coming toward him on Highway One had been real. He'd been buzzing from a few too many long-necks at the Corral, but he knew he hadn't just been seeing pink elephants.

He shivered as he reached his car. They had come at him with outstretched arms and what appeared to be blood on their lips.

"Keep away from me!" he'd screamed, whipping open the door.

He'd jumped in just in time, for they had immediately swarmed the vehicle, trying desperately to break in. They'd pounded on the hood and roof; they'd shaken the car up and down, howling. One had stuck its face up to the driver's side window and licked at him, leaving a cloudy smear of blood on the glass.

Keeping his wits, he'd started the engine and driven forward, pushing them away with the front of the moving car. The pawing, clawing creatures had been left stumbling in the wake of his exhaust.

At his first phone booth, he'd called 911. Surely the police would like to know that a band of psychos was running loose. But the dope at the station didn't buy a line of it and the tourist didn't really blame him.

"I wouldn't believe it, either," he said, getting into his car.

Starting his engine, he grumbled, "Gonna drive straight through to Atlanta." No stops! Even if his engine fell out and dragged on the pavement, he would drive until he was back in Atlanta. He wanted to put all the distance he could between himself and the Keys.

His eyes stared forward, and they looked right into a splotch of dried blood on the windshield. Disgusted, he turned on the windshield wipers and let them run for several minutes before turning them off.

He'd never be able to sleep again without his doors and windows locked.

Oblivious to the tourist's trauma, Sheriff Diggs sat back in his swivel chair and laughed with the dispatcher.

"You believe these kooks?" he said, chuckling so hard his belly shook. "Vampires? Hey, what are they servin' down at the Corral, anyway?"

CHAPTER 27

Devil's Deal

Like Sheriff Diggs, the vampires of the island were preparing to call it a night. Although they'd failed in snatching the tourist on the road, they'd devoured the fisherman.

They'd eaten. And that was a very good night indeed.

They were trudging back to their hideaways on the island when a boy stepped into their path.

Jeremy Wagner had altered his plan. He'd been eager to strike the deal with the vampires on Midsummer's Eve, but half the way home from Sawgrass Key, a disturbing thought had intruded and he had turned around.

He was sure the exchange—Mary and the kids—would be doable, but he did not know the true nature of the beasts on the island. What if they merely howled at him and ripped him to pieces, regardless of what he had to offer?

It would be better to go back and barter early. If they agreed, then all was set. If they killed him, then he would not have fallen before a group that thought he was invincible. It would be better to die alone.

The first vampire, John Lee, snarled, "Kill him!"

"Wait!" Jeremy shouted; holding up his hands

in the sign of a cross. Since all he knew of vampires came from movies and books, it was all he could do.

"Wait? For what, son of the living?" John replied, licking his lips.

"I know about the curse," Jeremy said, backing away. The hair on his neck was standing.

It was real. Everything the diary had said was true. But even in his excitement, nothing—the entries, pictures, drawings, films, even the dream of freedom—could prepare him for the real thing.

From the darkness, these were the vampires of the legend, the night creatures who'd roamed the island for three hundred years.

"What do you know, boy?" John Lee grunted.

John Lee could sense the boy knew evil. That very evil which Jeremy radiated postponed a certain violent death.

"I know this," Jeremy replied, his voice wavering. "I know that a Jesuit priest was burned at the stake three hundred years ago and shouted to you, 'May God have mercy on your souls, but first may He condemn you to walk this island in search of your lost souls for three hundred years until Mary herself releases you.'"

"What else?"

"Who cares?" said another. "We eat the boy before he tells someone we're here."

The vampires began to move in on Jeremy.

"No!" John Lee stepped in front of Jeremy to protect him.

With the vampire so close, Jeremy fought a ferocious wave of nausea. The creature stank worse than anything he dreamed possible.

"I know about the Feast of the Dead," Jeremy continued, gagging between words. "I know about the great storm that swept the island after you killed the Indians."

"Go on," John Lee said, his back to the boy. His eyes drifted up to the sky. Deliverance? The strange boy and his knowledge excited him.

"And I know who Mary is," Jeremy said.

John Lee whirled around, seizing Jeremy by the shoulders. His words, passionately spoken in a foul breath, smote Jeremy's face.

"You do?"

Jeremy, pulling his head back, nodded.

The vampires stood silent. They may not have known or cared of anything else the boy spoke, but they knew the importance of the name. It was a faint point of light on the farthest edge of a black horizon.

For three centuries, all they'd known was sleep of the undead and eating; followed by the dark and running from the light; waiting perpetually for human flesh and blood.

Now, before them, was the first living human to speak the name since Father Menendez had cursed them.

He knew things about them that only they had known.

The vampires drew back.

They'd seen progress over 300 years and had begun to understand that it was only a matter of time before they were exposed, hunted down and slain—forever damned. Although an army of six, they would falter before their twentieth-century adversaries.

"Tell us what you know, boy," John Lee said. "Tell us everything."

"I will," Jeremy whispered.

And so Jeremy revealed all he had learned. While there were a million things he wanted to extract from them, he realized it was a time of telling, not of asking.

He had to fill their ears with what they yearned to hear. As he spun his story, the vampires stared to the sky in longing.

He sensed he was gaining their trust. And in order to live forever, he would have to have it.

After he'd finished his story, he looked around and spotted the blood-spattered Toyota Land Cruiser. He gulped, thinking back to the hand-print on the boat.

His eyes returned to the vampires. Lost in their dreams, they appeared vulnerable. It was time to make his move.

"I know you always need food," Jeremy start-ed. "But all I ask is that you be patient for two more nights, and then I will bring you more food than you could ever dream of. There will be so much that it will last you for weeks."

The vampires stared at him in disbelief. Where would this boy get food?

"I will have so many people here that you will be able to have your Feast of the Dead in grand fashion," Jeremy continued.

The looks on their faces made Jeremy confident that his plan was working.

Suddenly, one vampire's expression turned ugly. He stepped forward, rage spreading across his face like a destructive fire.

"No!" he screamed. "The boy is lying!"

Jeremy laughed. "If you don't believe me, I will bring you a sample before the feast. Just to show you what I can offer."

The vampire growled. "No! We are pirates! We do not accept offerings! We take what we want!"

"Once they hung pirates, now they'll hunt you down and burn you out if the truth be known," Jeremy replied, cool as ice. He crossed his arms on his chest.

Yes. Yes, it was working.

"Bring us one!" one of the others called out.

Knowing full well who he would serve up, he grinned. "Fine. I will bring you a boy."

Billy Peters. Billy Peters, who stared at him like he knew and hated what Jeremy was into.

Billy Peters, the goody-two-shoes who ridiculed Jeremy's looks and heavy-metal music.

"When?" the vampire asked.

"Tomorrow night."

"How can we be sure? How do we know you're not going to bring the living back to destroy us?"

"You're just going to have to trust me," Jeremy said, smiling the smile of a salesman who's just made the sale of his life. "There will be so much more. In two nights, the roads will be filled with teenagers. If you believe in me, you will have more than you can imagine."

John Lee stepped forward and lifted Jeremy off the ground. "What about Mary, boy? What about Mary?"

Jeremy sensed immediately that this was indeed what would close the deal. He could see it in John Lee's desperate eyes.

"Leave Mary to me," he said coolly. "You'll have her. Now put me down."

John Lee lowered him. If it had been any other person, he would have already gutted him. But this one offered a promise of salvation.

Jeremy brushed his arms, where some of the vampire's crumbling decay and filth had dirtied his shirt and skin.

John Lee stepped back, his eyes scanning the boy up and down.

"And what is in this for you, boy? Why do

you bring this to us?"

Jeremy nodded, looking each one of them over. With carefully chosen words, he said, "I want your Feast of the Dead to set me free. I want to live forever."

"This is what you want?" John Lee replied, motioning toward himself and the others. "You want to live like us?"

"No, no," Jeremy said, laughing at their apparent ignorance. "Not like you. Pardon me, but you guys stink like hell. I'm going to live a cool life forever. I'm gonna fly the world, explore countries I've never seen, pick up chicks from all corners of the globe."

John Lee's eyes bore through Jeremy. He knew the boy did not understand the pain of their life after death.

"And what if you are wrong, son of the living?"

"I know I'm right. I know it." Jeremy stood confidently before the vampires. His purpose was set. "And if not, then I'm dead. But even that will be better than knowing that someday I'm gonna be a rotting corpse. I'll take my chances."

John Lee shook his head. The boy was foolish.

"So that's the devil's deal we'll strike, okay?" Jeremy said to him.

Without a contract to sign, Jeremy concluded

his business the only way he knew how. He stuck out his hand.

Hesitantly, confused, John Lee extended his own.

As they gripped, a pain unlike any other he could explain shot through Jeremy. Deep in the background of his greed, his soul screamed. He beat it into submission.

John Lee's smile broke wide after he pulled his head back. He had only one word on his mind.

Release. Release from the prison of eternal life in the world of the undead.

Jeremy soon remembered that Tina was to meet him at midnight. He would have to burn tracks to get there on time. But if he didn't, *c'est la vie.* He was concluding the single most important exchange of his lifetime.

He turned to leave. "Tomorrow you get the boy. At the Feast of the Dead, you'll have food and you'll have Mary.

"And then you set me free."

John Lee nodded. He watched the strange young boy move away in the direction of his car.

The vampires stood in silence for some time, listening only to the waves crashing against the beach.

The end was near.

CHAPTER 28

Nightmares

Mary woke from her sleep and called out to Tina. When Tina didn't answer, she looked at her cousin's bed—empty.

Figuring her cousin had gone downstairs to get a glass of water, Mary closed her eyes and let her head fall back to the pillow.

The soft swish of the trees moving in the wind outside soothed her. Snug in her blanket, she smiled. After all that had happened, she actually felt some peace.

She drifted back toward peaceful slumber. But from somewhere deep in her dreamworld, she heard a voice that startled her.

Mary.

Mary's head snapped up from her pillow.

Her heart beat wildly, her skin felt clammy in a sudden cold sweat. She scanned the room, waiting for something or someone to jump out.

Drawing up her legs, she pulled her blanket tightly around her and huddled against the headboard.

At the south end of Sawgrass Key, where the captain of USAir 558 had met his death, the stillness of the night was deafening.

Drawing closer to Vampire Island, all that

could be heard was a strange, terrible moaning. The vampires, sitting in a circle on the beach, voiced their pleasure of a promise of the future.

They had fed that night, and now there would be more. A boy had promised food, enough to raise their spirits. And if he came alone without what he had sworn to deliver, then he would simply take the place of what he'd failed to fulfill.

They were not the only ones thinking of Mary.

Jeremy drove home down Highway One, music blasting out his open windows. The jet of air that blew his hair back felt invigorating. He had brought his plan to fruition, and now all he could think of was Mary.

He sent his thoughts out to her. Mary would be his ticket to eternal freedom. Mary would be the sacrifice offered in his mad pact.

The yearning for Mary gathered force as thoughts and dreams joined to drift out across the islands and waters.

Mary, Mary.

The sound penetrated barriers and obstacles, wafted over trees and roofs, entered homes and rooms.

But most of those in Marathon slept deep in the sweetness of slumber and did not hear.

There was only one ear, one mind, which it sought.

Mary shot up from sleep and bolted upright, frightened and trembling. The voice from the airport came back to her anew. She heard the same voice, and more.

She thought she was going crazy.

The voice. The boy at the airport, the one outside the house. The occult.

Based on what she knew, all pointed toward one dark figure: Jeremy.

Most likely, he'd been the one at the airport. And he was probably the one speaking to her now.

But she couldn't be sure.

The voice came to her again, soft and seductive. It lulled her to sleep like a potent anesthetic.

In her dream, she danced with the boy from the black car. A fire burned wildly in the center of a circle, and Indians shrieked and ululated, carrying skeletons and decaying bodies in an orgy of death. The boy let go of her hand and ran toward the fire. He urged her forward.

Mary shook her head. "No! Leave me alone!" Yet he pulled her on.

Powerful, he controlled her mind, her thoughts. She was helpless to his resolute commands. He owned her, and what he said was law.

She followed him to the top of a huge hill of sand—one of the great burial mounds—where they stood high above the wild dance. Taking her hand, he began to speak of things she could not understand.

"Release them," he whispered into her ear. When her face registered confusion, he pointed out beyond the dance to six lone figures wandering aimlessly near the edge of the beach.

"What are they?" she asked, shuddering. Watching them was simultaneously saddening and terrifying; she had to turn her face away.

With her eyes closed, she could hear the beginning of their cries.

Mary, Mary, MARY!

"They are waiting for you," he said.

"But who are they?"

"They are vampires, creatures of the night. They have waited three hundred years in agony for you, Mary. For you to come and release them."

"Release them?" she said, dizzy. "We should kill them."

He gripped her wrist with his other hand. "No. They are suffering and you have the power to set them free this very night."

"But why? Why should I? How?"

"We can live forever," he said, his voice seductive. He squeezed her hand tightly.

"What are you talking about?"

"If you set them free, you will live forever. With me. The king and queen of eternity."

He began to laugh, a shrill, insane sound that pierced the night sky. It went on and on, growing louder and louder, until...

Mary shot up from her cot again. Sweating and crying, she cupped her face in her hands.

She sobbed, horrified and confused.

"Why...why me?"

Her prayers that it was all only a bad dream crumbled as she heard her name floating through the air of the room.

Mary, Mary, MARY!

She didn't care anymore about Tina's stupid ceremony or Jeremy; the icy rain of her fear had extinguished the curiosity which had burned but an hour before.

She just wanted to feel like a normal teenage girl, one who thought about boys and vacation and fun, not death and sadness and evil. She wanted out. Yet, the ocean of voices surrounded her and seemed to box her in.

CHAPTER 29

Black Arts

Shortly after Tina snuck out the back door of the house, Elly Tipton's eyes opened. She'd been sleeping in her rocking chair, Bible clutched to her chest to protect her from the evil all around her.

Her eyes foggy from sleep, she couldn't make out the shape on the sidewalk beneath her window. But whatever it was looked up at where she sat, and she swore it had spoken to her, causing her to wake.

Draping her shawl around her shoulders, she walked down the dark stairs and out the front door. The air outside was fresh compared to the thick, asphyxiating air of evil in her house.

She stood at the edge of the porch, looking at the man. Whoever it was did not frighten her; whoever it was seemed an ally.

A floating chorus of voices stirred the wind and the trees. Both she and the man looked up as they heard the sounds:

Mary, Mary, Mary.

She looked at him.

"The girl is evil," she said. "I know she's one of Satan's children."

The man nodded his head. Taking a deep breath, he moved toward her.

He truly believed that these things were happening because God had steered him to this mission. Everyone was a link in the chain leading to this final confrontation: the woman at the church, the cabdriver, and now the woman from the house.

When they were standing face-to-face, Elly saw he was a holy man. She nodded her head, her eyes telling him he had her trust.

Reverend Moses opened his Bible and whispered a prayer of hope: "For God hath not given us the spirit of fear; but of power, and of love, and of a sound mind."

His eyes probed her, searching for the despair that lay within.

"I have felt your pain; I know your pain," he said.

"How could you know what I have been through?" was all she could respond.

"Because I too have lost a loved one. I was walking down the street when I heard you from that window. I understand. We've both lost to the darkness someone precious."

"The spirit of God is strong within you," she said. "You are a true believer."

Reverend Moses nodded. "I believe in things I've seen, things I haven't seen, and things I know I will never see. I also know this: Evil has come to your island."

"Come and sit," Elly said, motioning toward

two chairs on the porch.

The two of them sat down, and Reverend Moses opened his Bible to Ephesians.

"You do understand that we must stand strong together. There is a great fight ahead of us. I always read this passage before I prepare to face down the faces of Satan: *For we are not contending against flesh and blood, but against the principalities, against the powers, against the world rulers of this present darkness, against the spiritual hosts of wickedness in the heavenly places.*"

Elly broke into tears, her head falling against his shoulder. "You know. You know they came and took away my baby."

"I know there is a lot of evil in this world, and I have been told of the agents of darkness right here on this island. Tell me what happened to your little one. Tell me where they might have taken him."

A late summer chill made Tina draw her coat tighter. She would have preferred waiting inside Jeremy's house rather than on the back porch.

"I hope he gets here soon," she whispered to herself, shivering as she watched the shadows of the trees against the house.

Minutes later, she heard the engine of his Black Cat as it pulled slowly into the driveway. The car door slammed, and Jeremy walked around the house.

"I knew you'd come," he said.

Looking at him, she didn't know whether to hug him or hate him. "What was so important that I had to come out at this time of night?" she asked, irritated.

"I wanted to see you, baby," he replied, running his hand through her hair. "I know I act strange sometimes, but I still care about you."

"Oh, Jeremy," Tina sighed. She was giving in to her feelings once again and Jeremy knew it. He capitalized on her moment of softness.

"Let's go to the gas station," he said. "I want us to call on Satan together, tonight."

Though she knew it was crazy, and aware that he was manipulating her again, she tried to resist his touch and the warmth of his voice.

She swallowed. "It's late."

"You want your mother to get better, don't you?" Jeremy seductively whispered in her ear.

"Yes," Tina responded. "I do."

They walked around front to the car, jumped in and drove off to Jeremy's dark place of worship.

Once at the gas station and inside, Tina sat on a bench against the wall as Jeremy left the room. Beside her were several of the books he used for summoning the gods of evil.

Her eyes could barely distinguish details but she knew without having to see; she'd been there enough times to know. There, on the wall in front of her, would be the hand-scrawled symbols and the satanic number 666 in black.

Her emotions shifted again. It felt so creepy, so *wrong?*

Once again she went over the reasons why she followed him, why she was there. She'd done it to be with him; she'd done it to cure the unhappiness that so often infected her life; she'd done it for her mother.

She knew that she wasn't any better off. She knew her life had become more troubling. And her mother?

Was her mother any better off?

She didn't think so.

So why do I keep coming?

Jeremy stepped back into the room. He wore a black robe and a wicked smile she'd never seen before. He was gloating over something. Exactly what, she had no idea.

He knelt in front of her, taking her hands in his.

"I've found the way to the other side, baby," he said, the smile never leaving his face. "The way to eternal life. You can come with me, if you'll just do as I say."

Tina stared back into his eyes, searching his soul for an answer.

CHAPTER 30

Morning

Like fresh rain that cleanses the earth, the summer sun bathed Marathon in its new light washing away many of the fears that accompany the night.

Mary stood on the front steps of Tina's house, feeling the intensifying heat of the waking day.

Her mind ran through the dreams and nightmares that had torn at her the night before. She thought of being in the house with Elly Tipton and it scared her.

She thought about Tina and Jeremy.

As she watched a boy toss newspapers from a speeding bike, her mind went back to the dream in which the Indians had danced, when her name was on the wind: *Mary, Mary, Mary.*

With so many things bothering her, Mary needed a friend. Tina wouldn't do; she was secure in her bed.

Tina was still out when Mary had fallen asleep for good the night before. Mary had begun to believe—did believe—that Tina had been out all night, not just wandering downstairs for a late-night drink.

The green perfume of summer swept through her nostrils, brushing her thoughts aside. She sat on the porch, raised her face, and enjoyed the warmth on her skin.

Several minutes later, Tina, dressed in a long blue T-shirt and cut-off shorts, came out the door with a cup of orange juice in her hand.

Mary turned to greet her. "Good morning, sleepyhead. Where in the world did you go last night?"

Eyes squinting to keep out the sun's blinding rays, Tina grunted. "Don't worry about it. Just lay off me this morning. I didn't get much sleep."

In fact she hadn't. Jeremy had been in rare form, keeping her up most of the night. His rituals had reached new heights, with Jeremy wild with excitement about having found eternal life.

Now it all centered around what he needed to do.

She looked over at Mary, who had her face tilted to the sun, her eyes closed.

"You must bring Mary to the meeting, Tina," he'd said. *"If there is any one thing you must do in this life, it is to be sure that you both come tomorrow night."*

Midsummer's Eve.

There was no way out now. By failing to overcome her feelings and her better judgment, she had committed to something unspeakable. There simply would be no way to escape from Jeremy's madness.

She'd tried to ask him if there was another

way—another way aside from having Mary with him to get what he needed.

"No, no way," he had said. In a moment of unusual bravery, she had demanded that he not go on about her cousin. It had really been giving her the creeps.

But he had turned on her, his eyes blazing hellfire. He had pinned her to the wall, his breath sour in her face.

"Don't screw this up, Tina," he'd said. "I swear, you better not let me down."

"And what if I do?"

He'd walked over to a small stack of books, pulled out a picture, and showed it to her.

It was a picture taken at one of their past meetings with everyone in black robes kneeling around a pentagram on the floor. There was one bright, pretty face that showed most clearly: Tina's.

"I swear, Tina, if you don't come through for me, this picture will be everywhere: in the school, the newspapers, your family. Then everyone will know what you're into."

He had her, and there was no way she could fail to bring Mary without having her life on the island completely ruined.

"Come on, kiddo," she said to Mary. "Let's go for a ride today. Let's roll down the windows and let the guys check us out."

The idea sounded great. Perhaps it really was

the start of a brighter day.

"Awesome!"

They giggled as they ran to the Mustang.

"With my luck, this will be a geek holiday in the Keys, with parades and banners and buttons and the whole shebang," Mary said, the corners of her mouth turning up.

When they were both inside the car, Tina started it up. She shrugged. "I guess when you get right down to it, all boys are geeks. They're just packaged differently."

Mary said the next in good humor although it made Tina cold.

"Is that true for Jeremy? Is he a geek, too?"

Tina thought about Jeremy ranting around the gas station in a black robe, jabbering about the devil and eternal life.

After she'd pulled out of the driveway, she replied, "You can judge for yourself tomorrow night."

CHAPTER 31

Billy Peters

Late that morning, Sheriff Diggs entered the station streaming a trail of obscenities behind like exhaust. He'd been drinking late the night before, and he hated to work!

"Mornin', Sheriff," the dispatcher said, stifling a giggle.

"Shut up," Diggs replied, pouring himself a cup of black coffee. "Just shut up and leave me alone."

He sat down and looked at his cluttered desk, on top of which was a phone message from the Coast Guard.

Cursing his hangover, he grabbed the phone to return the call.

The man on the other line relayed the results of the previous night's search for the missing German tourist. Sheriff Diggs responded with several *uh-huh*s between the thudding of a headache.

The search had turned up empty.

"Well keep lookin'," Diggs said. "The guy rented a boat. You boneheads at least can find the boat!"

"We'll do what we can," the man replied.

"Darn right you're gonna do what you can. You're on taxpayers' time. One begins to wonder whether or not you boys are spendin' too much time playin' cards or somethin'."

Agitated and offended, the man on the line hung up.

The fact that Diggs too was on taxpayers' time was different, of course. The Coast Guard was federal, and he was local. To Sheriff Diggs, that was a rather large distinction that could not be overlooked.

The sheriff kicked his feet up onto his desk and pulled his hat down over his eyes. No matter what else happened that day, he would be sure that the blame for that particular issue would fall on anyone but him.

But there were others on the island who had contrary feelings when it came to the subject of blame and where it rested. One of those people was working at Peters' Bait and Boat Shop, deliberating an opportunity to redeem a previous wrong.

Billy Peters had worked the previous summer at his uncle's store, where he had made a healthy five dollars an hour. Not the U.S. Treasury, but enough to keep money in a high-school boy's pocket.

Late in the summer, several boys he knew from school had begun shoplifting items from the store. Billy, torn between helping his uncle's business and losing friends, had pretended ignorance.

After his uncle had taken inventory and noticed the missing merchandise, he'd singled out his nephew, who'd been in charge of running the shop on slow days.

The blame for such a substantial amount of missing goods fell on Billy. His uncle blamed him for failing to stop the thefts, an offense in Hank Peters' eyes equal to Billy stealing the stuff himself.

Thinking he'd lost his uncle's favor, Billy had taken the job at the airport. But when his uncle asked him back to work part-time for the summer, Billy received a shot at redemption.

And after Jeremy Wagner walked out, Billy Peters felt he had an even greater chance at redemption.

Billy'd been in the back when he'd heard the bells. Coming out, he'd seen Jeremy standing in front of the counter.

Knowing there was never any love lost between them, Billy had been apprehensive at first.

"What d'ya want, Jeremy?" he'd said, tensing himself for a confrontation.

Jeremy had tried to calm him. "Listen, Billy. I know we don't like each other very much, but we can try to get along."

Billy's eyebrows went up. "What are you up to, Jeremy?"

Jeremy'd laughed. "Cool down, cowboy. I

just wanted to pass somethin' on to you. I was down by Sawgrass Key to do a little swimming when something moving caught my eye. When I got a little closer, I saw it was a boat."

Jeremy popped a cigarette into his mouth.

"Well, then I got to thinkin' that there's been a whole ruckus comin' up from your uncle about a missing boat. I put two and two together, and I thought I'd come and tell you that I'd seen one. Maybe it's yours."

Billy stared closely at Jeremy, trying to detect foul play. When Jeremy dragged on his cigarette and smiled innocently, Billy relaxed. Regardless of Jeremy's motive, it was an opportunity to make good with his uncle.

"Well, where is it?" Billy'd asked.

"Not so fast, hot shot," Jeremy replied, cool as a reptile. "It's in a place that's kind of hard to find, so I think it'd be best if I went with you, 'cuz I know just about right where it is."

"Well, when are we gonna go then?"

"I have some important stuff to take care of during the day, so I most likely won't be able to come back until later this evening."

Then he added, "After sundown."

Now Billy was hashing out the whole scenario.

What was the best possible way to present his find to his uncle? Going back to Sawgrass Key with Jeremy would throw the heroics onto Jeremy's shoulders, for he was after all the one who'd seen it. That would make Billy second-hand news.

But what if he went out there right now? Brought it back to Uncle Hank by himself, claiming it was his find? That surely would earn him a higher mark.

He wouldn't wait until Jeremy came back. He would go find the boat and proudly return it.

He knew the general area Jeremy'd described, so trudging through the water and scrub wouldn't be all that bad.

Billy waited until his uncle came back from lunch. He didn't stop to get a sandwich or pause for even a sip of water. He jumped into a skiff parked at the dock and pushed off toward Sawgrass Key.

To his surprise, he hardly had to look at all. After several minutes of searching, he guided his skiff toward the lagoon, where the capsized boat was bobbing near land.

"Hot dog!" he yelled out, maneuvering around a fallen palm.

When close enough, he leaned over and pulled the boat toward him. The number on the metal tag was the same as the one that'd been missing.

The boat was indeed close to land, so he wouldn't get more than waist-wet turning it upright. But the idea of jumping into that murky water made him squeamish.

Perhaps he should just go back to the shop and tell Uncle Hank that he'd found it? That would still earn him some merit.

But then he caught sight of the bloody handprint. Scratching his chin, he stared at it. "What the...?"

He looked around the lagoon, debating how to proceed with this new discovery, when he saw yet another mystery: a four-wheeler with the driver's door wide open.

Billy steered his skiff toward the opposite bank. He tied it up and jumped onto the dry land.

"Hello?" he called out. He spoke more from nerves than from curiosity.

When no one answered, he crept toward the door. A third puzzle then came into sight.

Yet another bloody handprint, a fresher one than on the boat.

"What the heck's been goin' on around here?"

He began to pace, his hands in his hair. "Oh, man. Oh, man. What am I gonna do?"

He stepped toward the vehicle and peered inside. Nothing unusual, just some bags and some gear on the backseat. And from the bugs crawling on the front seat, the door had been left open for some time.

Billy backed away, taking another whole look

at the Toyota. Aside from the handprint and the trails of blood on the door, there was no other sign of damage. The tires were not flat, the hood wasn't up.

"This ain't no car trouble," Billy said, his skin bursting with goose bumps. "Some real trouble happened here."

He thought of calling the sheriff—understood it was the proper thing to do—but then his internal defenses kicked in.

He well knew the consequences of blame; he'd already been in that situation.

Surely lazy-butt Sheriff Diggs would find a way to pass the buck onto Billy Peters; the short, fat arm of the law had a way of doing just that to folks regularly.

No. Not this time.

There would be no more blame dropped on Billy Peters' shoulders. He'd learned his lesson.

He thought about what his uncle would tell him. Uncle Hank Peters, who had so much invested in his boat, would say grab the boat and leave the rest to the cops.

Billy darted back to his skiff and untied it. He moved to the capsized boat, and, ignoring his feelings about the water, jumped into the lagoon. Using handfuls of sand and water, he scrubbed the handprint until it started to fade.

He tied it to his skiff and headed back to the marina.

On his way back, Billy Peters stood proudly, sucking in the salty Gulf air through his nose. He felt strong, refreshed, and most of all, redeemed.

The blame would be lifted from his shoulders.

Blame would change hands that very day. From Billy's redemption would come Jeremy Wagner's condemnation.

When Billy pulled his prize into the dock behind Peters' Bait and Boat Shop, the sun was still high in the sky, moving westward.

High in the sky, too bright for certain creatures to come out and feed. And when they did come out there would be little to feed upon.

And for that lack of food, the vampires on Vampire Island would have plenty of reasons for hunger, and one person to blame.

CHAPTER 32

Calling Satan

Midsummer's Eve

Tina could feel the remaining minutes of her normal life ticking away. She watched Mary apply lipstick in the mirror over her dresser.

They'd been able to make the best of the previous afternoon, driving down to the beach and soaking up some sun. The two girls had even been able to meet a couple of interesting guys who had talked with them and bought them sodas.

Tina's mind paused on that boy and she yearned for the life of a regular teenage girl. Instead of the wonderful freedom of adolescence, her life was filled with suffocating problems.

Her conscience bothered her. She had brought up the subject of stopping by Jeremy's party at some point in the evening, and had detected some apprehension in Mary's response.

All dressed up, the girls prepared to leave. Mary stood at the door while Tina ran dinner up to her mother.

Elly Tipton smiled when her daughter entered with food. She thanked Tina for the meal and stared after her as she said good-bye.

As she walked down the stairs, Tina began to

recognize that her mother had seemed uncharacteristically content. The thought rattled her. But as she closed the door, all else was forgotten. On to Midsummer's Eve.

The girls started out the evening by stopping at one of the several parties raging on the beach. They flirted and drank in front of a blazing bonfire before Tina popped the question, "Should we go now?"

Mary looked at her. "I don't know, this is kind of fun," she said reluctantly.

Tina could literally feel Jeremy waiting. "But the meeting will be starting real soon."

Mary agreed. "Okay."

They returned to Tina's Mustang and drove across town to the old gas station, Tina's heart pounding furiously the whole way. What was going to happen to her? What was going to happen to Mary?

The girls were leaving behind the best party of the entire year. For what? It wasn't as though they were going to a concert or rave dance, both of which might have been good excuses to split.

They were going to a cult meeting.

All Tina could hope as they pulled into a hidden space behind the gas station was that somehow they could make it through the night and that somehow she would finally be free of Jeremy Wagner.

The dry grass behind the building crunched

beneath their feet as they walked in silence. Before they came to the back door, Tina grabbed Mary's arm.

"Listen, Mary, we don't have to go in if you don't want to, really," she said, knowing full well that they had to. Jeremy had her in a tough spot, one from which she could not escape.

"No," Mary replied. "It's okay, really."

Tina dropped her head and opened the door. *Please God. Please let everything be okay. Please.*

They entered the room, their eyes blinking in the thick smoke of incense and flickering candle-light.

Mary noticed strange symbols on the walls. She noticed a strange congregation of people milling around in the dark room: poor kids, very poor kids. Judging by the group's attire, most were poor.

Suddenly it dawned upon her that she had stepped into something that went beyond rumors and tabloid articles.

Just two days ago she wouldn't have believed she would do such a thing.

With her fairly fluent knowledge of Spanish from high school, she was able to interpret some of the incantations rising from the worshipers at the far end of the room.

Trying to absorb all the strange things around her, she could not help but wonder where Jeremy was.

In a separate room, Jeremy pulled on his black robe. The girl was there: He could feel her. It would soon be time. Freedom was so close that he could almost touch it with his fingers.

The jerk Billy Peters had thrown a monkey wrench into his plan by disappearing when Jeremy returned to Peters' Bait and Boat Shop to find him. He'd slammed his fist on the closed door, cursing the day Billy was born.

When his temper had calmed, he'd driven back home hashing over how he would explain not bringing Billy to the island. He surely could not have gone back himself with an excuse. He would just have to hope that what he would bring them that night would be enough to make the vampires forget.

He drew his hood over his head, smiling and thinking of Mary.

Mary sat on a bench, stunned. She'd never seen anything quite like it.

The people murmured and chanted

Tina, who sat next to her, nudged her. "Can you see okay?"

It's fine," Mary replied, not taking her eyes away from the bizarre scene.

Tina closed her eyes, trying desperately to imagine a scenario in which she and her cousin would walk away.

She couldn't believe she was actually at a black

ritual. It was scary, yet it fascinated her. It was like the strange, different, unexplored things seen on "Geraldo."

"When do they start?" she asked nervously.

Her mind began to tell her that she might actually enjoy it, almost commanded her to do so.

Oh, Mary, it's gonna be so groovy.

It was the voice. That same voice spoke out. She looked around, and seeing that no one else paused to listen, she knew she'd been the only one to hear.

But in that room, in that world which she'd entered, it no longer seemed strange. For some odd reason, she suddenly no longer felt afraid.

While Mary slowly relaxed, Tina increasingly fidgeted, waiting for the moment when Jeremy would present himself.

A sudden movement of gathering people indicated the formal ceremony would begin. The others fell silent as the worshipers began chanting and shuffling around.

Once it began, the entire group was mesmerized. Mary watched the event with dumbstruck wonder. Her skin broke out in a cold sweat as she anticipated what would happen next, and she was soon lost in the hypnotic droning of the performance.

Jeremy peeked from the hallway into the room. He spotted Mary next to Tina and smiled as he watched her fixation. It showed in her face. He could tell.

"Oh, Jeremy, pal," he whispered to himself. "This is better than you could have imagined. She actually likes it!"

She was hooked! He could tell. He would goad her on as much as he could. She would go to Vampire Island—of that he was sure. He wouldn't have imagined it, yet she appeared to be transfixed by the events around her.

He called to her in his thoughts. The evil in him felt stronger than ever, his voice more articulate than any other time he'd spoken.

Tonight's the night, Mary.

From the shadows, he saw Mary turn from watching. She was the only one in the room to move.

The voice had penetrated her mind.

Mary. Feel it. Feel the power. This night is yours.

Mary suddenly stood up, shaking her hair out loosely. She felt primitive, nasty, bestial.

"Mary!" Tina said in a hoarse whisper. "What are you doing?"

"I want to be part of it," Mary replied.

Mary walked until she was in the middle of the circle. The satanists kept their ceremony going, although they looked at her with questioning faces.

It's okay, Jeremy said to them. *She is special.*

She will do as she pleases.

Tina watched in horror as Mary methodically moved through the steps of the ceremony. She wanted so badly to grab her cousin's hand and run, but they were in too deep. There would be no turning back.

Finally, Jeremy made his grand entrance.

He'd barely stepped into the room when all fell silent. All eyes went to the makeshift curtain. The flickering candlelight caught the silhouette of a man.

Jeremy could feel the threat resonating in the air. A power stronger than the thrill of blood and death had broken the spell over the room.

A slight breeze from the door beyond pushed through, rustling the curtain and throwing the candles' flames back and forth.

In desperation, Jeremy willed Mary to turn to him.

She heard his beckoning and slowly turned her head. Her eyes locked on Jeremy's while the congregation watched the curtain.

A low, steady voice full of purpose swam into the room from behind it.

Mary pulled her stare from Jeremy back to Tina.

"Suddenly a voice behind the curtain interrupted the ceremony. "You will not give your life to evil!

Jeremy was frightened. Never before had

someone intruded. And whoever it was, he surely meant to bring Jeremy down. If the man was not alone, the cops would surely be there soon. His hideaway had been discovered.

He fled.

Mary turned to the man. She saw a big, black, calloused hand pull the curtain aside.

A few feet behind him stood Elly Tipton.

Reverend Moses had believed that one way to find his enemies would be through the troubled youth on the island. He'd felt it soon after he'd begun to scour the island for information, and the belief had been confirmed when he'd heard Elly howling from her upstairs window.

Listening to her words, the reverend had been sure the good Lord, through Elly, had sensed something amiss in the young girls. Acting on that belief, he'd convinced her that following the girls would steer them toward the inevitable, necessary confrontation.

And he had been right.

Elly stepped forward.

"Mother," Tina whimpered, feeling faint.

"Oh, Tina," her mother said, opening her arms. "Come to me. I'm here to help you." She moved past the confused crowd of kids, to her daughter. "Tina, please come with me. I won't lose another child to evil. I love you."

As Jeremy bolted through the trees and weeds behind the gas station, he could hear the man's voice ring into song as he preached from the Bible.

The sound assaulted his ears.

He reached his car and dug into his pockets with shaking hands.

"Oh man, oh man," he said in a cracking voice. He turned the key in the lock of the Black Cat. "I've got to get to the island. Got to warn the vampires they're here."

He revved the engine and pulled out, shooting out a spray of gravel and loose dirt. He ripped past the gas station to the road. He was safe for the time being, and glad to put some distance between him and the holy man.

But he had not forgotten his prize. Everything had turned drastically wrong—he would have a lot of explaining to do—but all hope was not yet lost. There was still Mary. The vampires would still want Mary if nothing else.

Before he had driven too far away from the disaster, he sent out a desperate message. He knew she had to hear him.

The bridge, Mary. Meet me under the bridge. Escape them and join me. They are trapping you. They are going to turn you in.

He stuck his head out of the window and howled at the stars, the night, and the freedom that lay just beyond the end of his rainbow, which fell on Vampire Island.

CHAPTER 33

Reverend Moses

Mary stood rooted to her spot, struck dumb and unable to move.

Her mind swam in confusion. Two opposing forces pulled at her and she felt caught in a spiritual tug of war.

She had heard Jeremy's command, and it had been strong, but now that he was gone, his power faded. Now she could only face what was left: a strange black man in a white robe who talked of God and salvation.

The remaining congregation, feeling trapped in the middle of a mammoth confrontation, quietly dissipated.

Tina sat weeping on the bench against the wall, her mother embracing and rocking her.

Reverend Moses moved farther into the room and reached for Mary. In a literal stupor, she could not resist. "Sweet child," he said, his voice thick, warm honey. "You must renounce this evil you have taken into your heart. The only road you'll travel will be pain."

Mary's world crumbled down around her. "I have done nothing," she said in a soft breath. The man's hand on her shoulder sent bolts of positive energy through her body, but there still remained enough of Jeremy's negative current to neutralize it.

Reverend Moses waved a hand through the room. "Look around you. This is all the devil's work. It is evil. It is wrong. You know that, don't you, girl?"

Mary opened her eyes and looked around, trying to see through his eyes. The room looked to Mary Knight like it would have two days ago, before she had been overcome by Jeremy's madness.

Before the voice, and Tina's talk of the occult, and Baby Eddie, and Aunt Elly, and a nightmare.

Behind Mary, Tina raised her face from her wet hands and looked at the stranger. She didn't know if he was truly there to save them.

And what about her mother, who hadn't left the house in years?

She glanced up to her.

"What are you doing here, Mom?"

"Oh, Baby," Elly replied, pulling Tina's head to her breast. "I came to help you. I have been a thorn in your side for so many years, and I've come to tell you you're not alone. The Lord spoke to me tonight, and he told me to love and cherish what I still have…you."

The reverend's eyes had been on Tina and Elly, but they moved back to Mary.

"I ask you, girl, will you fight Satan who has found his way inside of you?"

"Who are you?"

"I am Reverend Moses, and I've come to this island to cleanse it of the dark shadow under which it lies."

Mary stood calmly, her hands dangling at her sides. "I've done nothing wrong, Reverend."

And in truth, she had not. But what had she been about to do? The possible answer chilled her.

"I just wanted to see what it was like," she said, her mouth dry.

Mary continued to feel torn by her conflicting emotions. One thing that felt good, however, was Jeremy's receding hold on her.

"I'm talking to you, young lady!" the reverend's voice broke in.

Again her eyes wandered to the devil symbols and flickering candles that swayed in the breeze from the open door. She looked at the robes on the wall, at the makeshift black altar against the doorway.

Her life prior to two days before rushed up at her. Who she had been such a short time ago came to the forefront of her conscious.

What am I doing here?

"Did you hear me?"

"Yes, Reverend. I know you're talking to me." Her own voice came back, but it still sounded somewhat faint, calling out from a foggy distance.

Gradually, this night's frenzy passed. Soon she was Mary Knight of Orlando, home of Mickey Mouse and his pals.

Through a tongue like cotton, she said, "I've never been to one before. I mean, I'm just a visitor."

The reverend grabbed her firmly by the shoulders. "You must leave Marathon. There is a great evil here, and that boy who just left is going to set it free."

They are suffering, Mary, and you have the power to set them free. Let them go this very night.

"Free to torment us. To haunt us. Condemn your evil ways!" The reverend held up his Bible.

Elly Tipton, looking respectfully upon the man, made the sign of the cross over Tina. She stood up and did the same in front of Mary.

The reverend lifted Mary's chin. "Do you know where the boy is going?"

Mary shook her head. "I'm not sure."

"Think, girl, think!" he shouted. He was close to the end of the long road he'd travelled, and the realization widened his eyes. "Your life and the lives of others depend on it!"

Mary closed her eyes and licked her lips. "He said, or I heard him say in my mind, to meet him under the bridge."

"Under the bridge?" the reverend repeated. His look went from Mary to Tina

Tina spoke up. "She means the bridge near

Sawgrass Key that leads down to Key West."

"Then that is where I must go," he said with resolution. Knowing that their share of the work had been done, he turned from them and briskly walked away, past the curtain and through the open doorway.

Mary moved halfway toward the door and called out, "Reverend Moses!"

But his ears were lost to her calling. All the sounds in the world could have called to him, and still he would have walked stiffly onward, toward the eagerly awaited confrontation with his enemy.

"Come on, Tina! Follow me!" Mary yelled, running after the strange man.

But nothing remained beyond the curtain but the dismal back room of an abandoned gas station and an open doorway that led to the dirt lot behind it. Mary poked her head through the door and looked right and left. No one could be seen.

"Where'd he go?" Tina said, coming up behind her.

The answer came from another voice.

Slowly, Elly Tipton joined the two girls in the doorway.

"He's gone to fight the evil ones. The ones who took my baby Eddie away."

CHAPTER 34

Final Battle

Reverend Moses walked through the trees behind the gas station until he came to the cab idling at a curb. The black driver, once so fervent a practitioner of Satanism, awaited the holy man behind the wheel.

The weight of Moses' words during his ten-dollar sermon had made the man a soldier in the reverend's army.

"Take me to the bridge," the reverend said, sliding into the backseat. "The one that heads toward Key West, the one near Sawgrass Key."

The drive turned to look at him. "Where's the woman?"

"I've left her behind. She's served her purpose. There is no need to throw her headfirst into the way of danger."

"What's at the bridge?" the driver said, pulling away from the curb.

"I believe that is where I will find them. If I am so lucky, I will finally confront the monsters that haunt this island and all the others."

"If you can call that lucky, Reverend," the driver replied, and the two men fell silent. The only sound to be heard was the tires against the pavement.

Mary and Tina, who'd bolted after Reverend

Moses, stopped at the curb short of breath. They watched as the car moved away.

Moments later, Elly Tipton appeared from the trees behind them.

Tina grabbed Mary's arm. "Come on, Mary! There's only one bridge south of here!"

Elly looked at Mary pleadingly. "Don't go, Mary! The evil ones have been calling your name. I've heard it in the wind."

Startled at her aunt's knowledge, Mary took a few seconds to reply. "I know," she whispered. "That's why I *must* go. A lot of what has been going on is because of me."

She looked back at Tina. "I'm going to take your car and follow Reverend Moses. Will you be able to get back home?"

"No way," Tina said. "You're not going alone."

"Look, Tina, I know you're afraid of what will happen to me, but you're going to have to let it fly. But there is something that has to be resolved that only I can fix. I don't know how, but if I don't go, then more bad things will happen."

Thinking of Mary facing off with Jeremy did not sit well with Tina, but she thought of all her cousin had endured since arriving. She thought of Jeremy's obsession with Mary, of the voices Mary said she'd heard. Tina had pulled Mary into the mess by asking her to come, but she no longer felt there was much she could do.

Mary would face her demons alone.

Signaling an unspoken acceptance, Tina turned to her mother. "Let's leave now, Mom. This place gives me the creeps."

"We'll find a way home," Elly replied. The look on her aunt's face made Mary believe that the woman knew much more about what was occurring than she'd ever admit. Perhaps she knew enough about good and evil on the island to realize what Mary had to face. "But first we have to take care of a few things."

Mary embraced her cousin and her aunt, then took the car keys and ran to Tina's Mustang. As she backed the car out, she saw Tina and Elly coming out of the gas station toting armfuls of Jeremy's satanic books and paraphernalia.

When only a block away down the main road, Mary could see in her rearview mirror the black smoke of a burning fire rising into the night sky.

Jeremy waited impatiently under the bridge. The growing storm blew with a fresh fury, and time was running short. He knew that soon he would be surrounded by adversaries.

"Man," he said to the howling winds, "she better get here real soon."

He closed his eyes and sent out a command to Mary.

He waited and waited. When he heard the

sound of approaching feet, he whipped his head around in relief.

His thought that he would see a young, pretty girl disappeared when a black man came into view.

Reverend Moses stopped at the bottom, staring into Jeremy's eyes.

"I am here, wicked little child," he said in a low, deliberate voice.

"Who are you?" Jeremy asked, his speech cracking.

"You are cursed with evil, boy," the reverend replied, stepping toward him. "I'm going to ask you to forsake Satan and all his evil, and that you save yourself before the inevitable casts you to hell."

Jeremy laughed. "Forsake yourself!" He then moved toward the reverend. "I'm going to live forever, old man!"

Reverend Moses shook his head. "Tsk-tsk. You young people think you've got it all. You're not going to live forever, boy. You're going to come with me."

The reverend took another step closer and Jeremy prepared for the battle.

Sheriff Diggs drove slowly along the back roads near the bridge. He sat comfortably now he knew the rising storm would spoil Midsummer's Eve and drive all the partying teenagers back home, away from mischief.

The night would have been smooth as fine linen had it not been for the call he'd received from Billy Peters.

Billy had returned the boat to his uncle's shop the day before in an attempt to hide from blame. The following day, struggling with guilt, Billy told his uncle the terrible secret, one in which someone might have died.

Billy then told the sheriff about the bloody handprint he'd found on the missing boat, and the sheriff had known immediately he had a problem on his hands.

He slowed his car to a crawl, turning his spotlight onto the scrub and trees surrounding Sawgrass Key.

"Dang kid said the Toyota was around here someplace," he said, chewing on the end of an unlit cigar. He shot his search beam through the palm fronds.

A great burst of wind kicked up sand.

"Jumpin' jackrabbits," he grumbled. "Storm's gonna be a bad one."

The vampires hid low beneath the moving beam. They'd crossed at low tide, and looking back behind them, they saw the wind had picked up considerably, the tide rising with it.

"We must go back," one of them said to John Lee.

"Silence," the leader whispered. "Just a little

more time."

His stomach grumbling, John Lee was famished. Thinking of his rage at the boy's lie about bringing food, he prayed the policeman would get out of the car. What a meal he would be.

When dark had fallen the night before, they'd risen in great joy believing they would be freed. They'd waited and waited, and then known they had been crossed.

They stared out at the cruiser with hungry, pleading eyes.

"Will we kill the boy when he comes?" one of the others asked, breaking the silence.

John Lee nodded. It had been some time since he'd felt such burning hatred. The boy he'd trusted, who knew so much about them, had tricked them. He'd told them lies so he could gather them together for a slaughter.

For three hundred years they had been successful in hiding from the living, except for the times when they killed. Many times, the challenge for survival had been reason enough to carry on.

That, and the need to eat, to please their insatiable appetites. Seeing the human mere yards away caused them all to remember that reason.

The storm grew even more furious, the trees and bushes bending before its onslaught. One of the vampires grabbed John Lee's arm: "If we don't go back now, we'll die!"

John Lee laughed as the winds pushed his skin against his face. "And what is wrong with that? Is that not what we want?"

Unaware of who was near him, the sheriff spotted the missing captain's vehicle and held his beam on it.

His pulse quickening, he got out.

The wind carried an offensive smell.

"Where's the road kill?" he called out, laughing in fear. The scent, Diggs thought, reeked of death itself.

If Sheriff Diggs had only known how right he was.

Jeremy used his weight to push Reverend Moses aside.

"Leave me alone!" he screamed, racing off toward Vampire Island.

"Come back!" the reverend shouted. "Ask for salvation while there's still time!"

"No!" Jeremy yelled. His desire to live forever still burned brightly inside him, and his main concern became warning the vampires that trouble had set foot near their hideaway.

Braving the storm, fighting to gain balance, Jeremy thought of how close Mary had come to serving herself up for his purpose.

There will be another Mary, he thought as he raced through the scrub palms.

Mary pulled from the road and parked near the bridge. She immediately saw Reverend Moses struggling up the slope.

"Did you find him?" she shouted. The wind tried to drown her voice.

"Yes," he panted. "But he ran away."

Another gust kicked sand in their faces. "Let's go back," he said, bending over. "It's too dangerous. We will find him tomorrow."

"No!" Mary shouted. "We have to find him tonight!"

She didn't know why she cared, but something inside of her wished to find Jeremy and stop him before tragedy fell. At that moment she did not wish that even Jeremy Wagner suffer.

Reverend Moses grabbed at her as she turned to run, but she was too fast. She sprinted down the same path Jeremy had taken.

"God protect you," he said, his voice blown away by a great gust of wind.

When he reached the end of the path, Jeremy saw the vampires hiding in the trees near the beach.

"Hey! Go back! Get back to the island!"

John Lee's head whipped around. He lurched out of the trees, his fangs bared.

He grabbed Jeremy and shook him.

"You lied! No boy ever came!"

The wind whistled in his ears. "I tried to get

him here. I might still have Mary!"

"Where are the many you spoke of...and where is Mary?"

"Hey!"

The voice startled them both. In a frenzy, Jeremy snared John Lee's soiled clothing and began shaking him.

"It's the cops! Run! Get back to the island!"

Sheriff Diggs came running toward them. "Who's there!" he shouted, aiming his flashlight at the two figures.

The other vampires came out to join their leader.

"What the heck?" Diggs said, stopping in his tracks. He though he recognized the boy, but he didn't have a magician's clue as to who—or what—the others were.

John Lee took Jeremy under his arm. "You come with us, traitor!" His strength was amazing as he carried Jeremy as lightly as a sack of groceries.

"No! Wait!" Jeremy shrieked. "Mary's here! I have to bring you Mary!"

Deaf to Jeremy's pleadings, John Lee retreated with his comrades. The storm knocked a palm tree over in front of them.

One of the vampires stuck his foul face in Jeremy's. "There is no Mary! But we have you!"

"But what about the Feast of the Dead?" Jeremy whimpered.

John Lee cackled as he hurdled the palm tree. The pounding rain soaked them all.

"There is no feast, boy! Can't you see! We're trapped forever! You will be our only feast!"

The sheriff ran after them. "Stop! Stop, or I'll shoot!"

But when he was within a dozen feet of them, he stopped cold. "Oh my God!"

"Help me! Help me, Sheriff!"

As if from nowhere, Mary came screaming. "Let him go! He's not the one you want! It's me! Here I am! I'm Mary!"

John Lee halted and turned. "Who is she, boy?"

"That's Mary!" Jeremy croaked. "She's the one you want! She can set you free!"

"As the one who has power over you, I command that you let him go!" she shouted at the top of her lungs.

"No," John Lee replied. "You tell lies. Mary has forsaken us."

They continued to head for their island.

"Wait!" Mary yelled. "Let him go!"

John Lee stopped and turned again. "Will you take his place? Will you join us to set him free?"

Their eyes locked and Mary was shocked to discover that she was not afraid of their horrible looks. She was not afraid at all. She could not allow the suffering to continue.

The other vampires looked out to the water and saw it was rising steadily. Time was running desperately short.

"Come now!" one yelled to John Lee.

"Save me!" Jeremy cried out, but John Lee's hold on him only grew tighter.

Mary ran forward. "Let him go!"

"Mary! Save me!" Jeremy screamed.

"Jeremy!" she cried back. "You have to promise you'll change yourself!"

"I promise! I promise!" he yelled as John Lee stepped into the saltwater separating the islands.

Still hoping they'd mistake her for their salvation, Mary pushed on. "Let him go or you'll never go free!"

Trudging the first few feet of violent, storm-churned water, John Lee turned and looked her in the eye. "No. We will never be free."

One vampire fell, almost swept away in the furiously rising water. Another helped him up.

Lightning lit the sky overhead, and rolling, booming thunderclouds moved menacingly closer.

Seeing them move farther away, Mary resorted to all she thought was left. She dropped to her knees and prayed for Jeremy's life to be spared.

The water rushed over Jeremy's head, causing him to spit out mouthfuls of it. "Please..."

"Shut your mouth, boy," John Lee snarled.

His legs grew heavy in the weight of the slamming waves.

"We'll never make it!" another cried.

"Don't worry!" John Lee called back. "Gracious death will never be our friend!"

The water came up to his neck, choking his words.

"But I don't want to live forever!" Jeremy sputtered.

John Lee used all of his strength to lift the boy over his head. "You won't!"

Those were the last words the vampire spoke before he and all the others began to disappear beneath the waves.

The storm exploded and Sheriff Diggs grabbed Mary, who cried and reached out toward Jeremy.

When they were back at the cruiser, Mary and Diggs both looked back.

They saw nothing but the waters that surged over Vampire Island.

Epilogue

No one who lived in the Keys had ever seen such a storm as the one that nearly uprooted them from their homes.

No one had seen it coming.

Many knew the legend surrounding the island across from Sawgrass Key; some others lived on in ignorance. But what they all knew was that the island called Vampire Island was no more.

But for the floating debris the storm had left behind, the island had been swallowed by the hostile waters of the Gulf of Mexico.

As time moved inevitably onward, the living found bits and pieces that suggested what might have happened there. Remains of ancient Indians washed up on the beaches of Marathon, and divers reported discovering bones and ax heads on the shallow Gulf floor where the island had been.

If indeed there had ever been vampires, nothing existed to prove it. Like the land on which they'd once stood, they'd been washed away, removed by forces of nature.

What had happened that last perilous night became the seeds of legend. And from that legend grew stories about the ultimate fate of the vampire creatures and the boy they abducted.

There were always those who took a more rational approach. Men like Sheriff Diggs believed that the people who'd been there that night had been drug dealers in disguise who had taken refuge on a boat and escaped the law.

As far as Jeremy Wagner's disappearance, well, that became Sheriff Diggs' solution to the missing tourist. His statement to the press screamed across the headlines shortly after: SATANIC TEEN KILLS TOURIST.

But there were those who knew differently, who knew the dark secret of that final, horrible night.

Mary knew otherwise. As did Tina. They had been to the edge of darkness and turned back.

There would be no happy nights for a long, long time. There would never again be talk of Baby Eddie, only silent memories. There would from that point on be a black spot that stained the bright, carefree days of youth.

But there was life.

Sweet, precious life, to be cherished for the rest of their time on earth.

And they would make the most of it because no one lives forever.

No one.

Don't Miss Derek Storm's Next Book!

Dead Zoo

COMING SOON!

Someone is hunting the children.
Someone who is a master hunter.
Someone who takes trophies.
Heads.

But someone with a video camera
caught him on the prowl.
Two teenagers who were just out having fun.
Now they're having the time of their lives…
trying to stay alive.
They don't want to end up in the Dead Zoo.